'Put it down,' I said. ~~~~~~~~~~~~~~~~~~~~~~~~~~ t
in here will take your head right off. Believe me.'

The white guy dropped his bat right away, although I
wasn't talking to him. The black guy thought about it,
hesitated, then did the same.

'Hands on the bar, both of you,' I said.

They obliged.

To JJ: 'Hold this.' I passed him over the pistol. 'It's a
shell, not shot. Aim for the chest. It'll make a hole big
enough to drive your car through. And watch it. It kicks
like a mule. I'll be right back.'

I bent down and picked up one of the axe handles. I
opened the door and went outside to the Blazer. I smashed
the windscreen, all the side windows, the back window,
both rear-light clusters, the head and spot lights, and the
wing mirrors, and snapped off the radio aerial.

A small crowd gathered at the bus-stop to watch, but
didn't interfere. The woman from the card shop next to
JJ's popped her head out of the door. 'Insurance job,' I
said. 'I'm the claims adjuster.'

I slung the handle through the broken windscreen and
went back into the bar.

Hearts of Stone

Mark Timlin

HEADLINE

First published in 1992
by HEADLINE BOOK PUBLISHING PLC

10 9 8 7 6 5 4 3 2 1

ISBN 0 7472 3844 8

Printed and bound in Great Britain by
Cox & Wyman Ltd, Reading, Berks

HEADLINE BOOK PUBLISHING
A division of Hodder Headline PLC
338 Euston Road
London NW1 3BH

For Mrs Lancaster,
who makes the best breakfast in London.

ACKNOWLEDGMENTS

Thanks and best wishes to:
Simon and Cathy Keable-Elliott, India and Jessie for letting me send them to Blackpool or Blackburn or somewhere like that to open a brasserie, and letting me convert Keable's Wine Bar into The Twist & Shout.

Steve Woolmington and the Ford Motor Company, for the loan of a Sierra Sapphire RS Cosworth 4x4, which unfortunately I had to return.

Adele Wainwright and Caroline Harris at Headline for coffee and sympathy.

Kerstan Mackness for taking all the digs about Arsenal.

And, of course, Hazel, with love.
Three years closer. Ai No Corrida.
Naijo No Ko.

Arms consultant: Arms De La Chasse, London.

1

I shut up shop in May. I'd had enough of the detective business.

It was no big deal. I just packed a few things in cardboard boxes, rented a garage to store them, locked the front door of the office, returned the keys to the estate agent, and paid off the lease. Simple.

I wasn't short of money, you understand. I had plenty. Enough, in fact, to pay off the mortgage on my flat. See, an old friend of mine had died and left me the sum of her worldly goods, including a rather pleasant terraced house in Brixton. I sold the place. I had considered living there myself, but I've got enough ghosts, thank you very much, without living somewhere where one more might walk the corridors on the dark midnight.

Then my ex-wife informed me that she, her new husband, their young son, and my daughter Judith were moving lock, stock, and barrel to Scotland. Aberdeen to be precise. About as far as they could go and still be in mainland Britain. My wife's new husband is a dentist, and apparently the teeth business is booming in that part of the world. It must be something to do with North Sea oil.

At first I did the aggrieved parent bit. You know the sort of thing. But, as my ex calmly told me, it wasn't as if they were leaving the country altogether. And anytime I was in the area I was welcome to pop in for a visit – I ask you. As if . . .

Of course, I eventually calmed down, and we sorted out

that I could see her during the school holidays and on her birthday and every other Christmas, and all that sort of malarkey. So it wasn't too bad. After all, I'd never been much of a father to Judith and, loath as I am to admit it, she'd be better off with her mother and her stepfather, who are rather better role models than I'll ever be. So that was that.

I've shed a few tears since she left, but sometimes I think they're much more for me than for my little girl, who'll be a teenager soon, and would probably have grown to despise me anyway. By the time she left, it seemed that everyone else I'd ever cared for had gone too. Even my cat seemed to prefer other digs.

I was like a ship that had lost its anchors. I floated where the times and tides took me. I went into a sort of decline. And it was nothing like I thought it would be. I didn't sit behind closed curtains in a filthy room, unshaven and eating TV dinners and watching porn videos on the box.

Did I, hell.

I shaved everyday. Shampooed and conditioned my hair, and checked the comb every morning to make sure I wasn't losing too much. I flossed my teeth, hoovered and dusted every other day, did two loads of washing a week in the Zanussi, and even ironed my T-shirts.

Every morning I took a stroll to the local café and breakfasted well, and exchanged merry banter with the staff and customers over my second pot of tea and the *Telegraph* crossword.

I slept alone. Not entirely by choice. The women I met sensed there was something not right about me. Probably that was just as well. You see, sometimes I'd come awake in the middle of the night calling out a list of the dead and dying who visited my dreams.

So that was me that summer. And as far as I was concerned, it would be me forever. But like all the

best laid plans, it wasn't to be.
You see, life goes on.

2

And as life went on for me, so it went on all around me, too.

Take the local bar that I drank in. The couple who owned it had sold up at the beginning of the year and taken themselves and their babies up north, where they opened a brasserie in Blackburn or Blackpool or somewhere like that. The old place was taken over by two ex-cabbies from east London, who decided that what was needed in the area was a tapas bar and Spanish restaurant. We, the locals, decided otherwise, and the new owners lasted just over three months. At almost the same time I closed my business, the bar was bought by a redundant advertising executive named Joe Jeffries. JJ to his friends. He was forty-something, with a surfer's haircut, a fitness fetish and a 1940s Willys station-wagon with wooden panels on the sides. He changed the name of the place to the Twist & Shout, or JJ's as it was known locally, stuck in a fifties Wurlitzer juke-box and an illuminated Budweiser sign, but otherwise didn't mess with the place much. That suited the locals down to the ground. We're a conservative lot in West Norwood.

I spent a lot of time in JJ's that summer, as May became June, which turned into July and then an August which started hot and dry with long, boiling days and short humid nights that brought threats of water rationing on the radio, as the trees turned crisp under the unrelenting sun, and all that could be comfortably worn was T-shirt and shorts.

5

Then the weather changed, and August leaked into September under a bloated leaden sky that would suddenly open without warning and let go rods of silver rain that bounced off the streets and pavements until the water ran like rivers in the gutters and carried brightly coloured litter and dog shit to block the drains.

One day in the middle of the month, when the lunchtime crowd had left and the evening crowd hadn't arrived yet, JJ and I were alone in the bar buying each other drinks and telling each other lies as usual. I was sitting on my regular stool at the corner of the bar in front of the big water-streaked plate-glass window and sucking on a bottle of Sol lager, and JJ was standing behind the jump, polishing a glass. The juke-box was playing a Ray Charles single, and all was right with the world. Suddenly the street door crashed open behind me and two geezers blew in, let it slam behind them, put up the CLOSED sign and pulled down the blind. I looked at them, and then at JJ, and he looked at me. One of the geezers was black, one was white, they were both young, bigger than average, and dressed in baggy street fashion. Although they could pretty well be described as average customers at the bar, average customers did not usually carry pickaxe handles. I looked over at JJ again, and he looked back at me and shrugged. I carried on drinking and he carried on polishing and we both waited for the punch-line. It wasn't long in coming.

'We're here for our money,' said the white guy.

'What money?' asked JJ, remarkably calmly under the circumstances.

'You know what money,' said the black guy and slammed his axe handle on the counter, destroying half a dozen or so plates that JJ had washed and dried but hadn't put away yet. 'Mr Lasky sent us.'

'Never heard of him,' said JJ, still calmly, and placed the glass he was polishing carefully on the bar in front of him. I did the same with my bottle.

'The money you pay us so that this sort of thing doesn't happen,' said the white guy and slammed the end of his axe handle against a particularly nasty mirror advertising a brand of Pilsner that the bar didn't stock anymore. I for one was glad to see it go, and I wondered for a moment if these two weren't from the good-taste police.

'Or this,' said the black guy and whacked my bottle of Sol a good'un so that it exploded and covered my nearly new Aquascutum trench coat, which I hoped made me look like Humphrey Bogart as Philip Marlowe, in a mixture of beer and broken glass. At that point I stood up. 'Sit down, cunt,' the black guy said, and smashed the stool next to mine into four or five pieces.

I sat down.

Now, if it had been a movie, JJ and I would have taken the pair of them apart and dropped them outside in the gutter and come back into the bar and had a celebratory glass each. But, being as it was real life, I sat, and JJ stood, and the two gangsters smirked at each other. Then the black guy looked at the juke-box, and tapped it gently on the glass bubble at the top with the lump of wood he was holding.

JJ went white under his sun-lamp tan.

'Leave it,' said the white guy. Then, to JJ, 'save yourself grief and pay up. We'll be back tomorrow, same time. We want a ton each, and no coppers or you'll be fucking sorry.'

I already was. I knew it was going to be murder to get the stains out of my coat.

The black guy ran his axe handle along the bar, sending everything on top on to the floor, then he and his partner left. I watched them get into a massive Chevrolet Blazer 4WD truck, sprayed bright red, and dripping with chrome, the black guy driving, and peel off into the traffic.

I looked at JJ, and he looked at me yet again.

'Was that for real?' I asked.

7

'Looks like it.'

'So who's Mr Lasky?'

He shrugged. 'Don't know. Do you?'

I shrugged back. 'Did you know they were coming?'

'If I had, I'd've baked them a carrot cake,' he said.

'They seemed to think you did.'

'There's been a couple of calls.'

'Threatening?'

'Vaguely.'

'Demanding money with menaces?'

'I suppose.'

'And you ignored them.'

'I get calls from double-glazing firms. I ignore them too.'

'If they start performing with those pickaxe handles near your window, maybe you'd better keep the phone numbers handy,' I said. 'You might be in the market for a spot of double-glazing sooner than you think.'

He just looked peeved and said nothing.

'Get me another beer, will you?' I went over and started picking up pieces of broken glass and china from the wooden floor. 'Got a dustpan and brush?' I asked.

Within ten minutes those two geezers might never have been inside the bar, except for the rapidly drying stains on my mac. We cleared up the mess, let up the blind, and turned the sign round again.

After the equilibrium was restored, JJ said to me, 'What do you reckon?'

'I reckon you should call Old Bill.'

'And end up with a set of busted windows like you said. Or worse.' He looked over at his beloved Wurlitzer.

'That's the risk you take.'

'You used to be in that game,' he said. 'What did you make of them?'

'Wankers,' I replied. 'Amateur night. They didn't even have a driver as look-out. They're just a pair of chancers looking for an easy score.'

'You want to help me out?' he asked.

'Not me, mate. I've finished with all that.'

'I'll buy you a new coat.'

I shook my head. 'I'll put it into Sketchley's. It'll be fine.'

'And I'll give you a job.'

'Do what? What do I want a job for?'

'You spend most of your time here anyway. You might as well get paid for it.'

That made as much sense as anything else I'd heard that afternoon. 'How much?' I asked. There was no harm in asking.

'Assistant manager. Four and a half an hour, plus a share of the tips, a decent meal and all the women you can pull. It's amazing how attractive they find barmen.'

'And a clean apron every day?'

'Every other day.'

What the hell, I thought. It was the best offer I'd had all year. 'You're on,' I said.

'What'll you do about those two, then?' he asked.

'You'll see. I'll come in tomorrow and deal with them.'

When I got home I went up into the crawl-space under the roof of the house and pulled out the last reminder of my previous life. I'd kept it for old times' sake, and this was exactly that – just like old times.

I felt around in the dark and pulled out a Holland & Holland 12-bore Howdah pistol almost old enough to be an antique. 1913 I think it was made. For an officer in the Indian army. The Howdah is a top lever, back action double-barrelled pistol, with an eight-inch barrel, pistol grips and exposed hammers. It looks something like a sawn-off shotgun, but the last two inches of the barrels are rifled, and it fires solid cartridges that can bring down an elephant. The whole thing wasn't much more than a foot long, weighed just over three pounds, and was sheathed in a custom-made holster with a leather bootlace threaded through two holes at the muzzle end, so that it could be fastened just above the knee and allowed the gun to be fast drawn like a revolver. The holster came with a matching belt, with leather loops to carry extra cartridges. The Howdah could be fired one-handed, but there was the risk of a broken wrist if you did.

I'd taken the gun and holster off someone I'd met whilst working on one of my last cases. It was a good weapon and was just what I needed to put the fear of God into the pair of would-be protection racketeers I'd met earlier. There was half a dozen of the heavy, pointed shells in a box next to the gun. I took just two: they were all I'd need, and I hoped I wouldn't actually have to use either of them. I took the gun down into my flat and dusted it off and broke it down and cleaned it, dry fired and loaded it. I put on the rig and slid the gun into its holster, and pulled on my Aquascutum. There wasn't even a bulge to show it was there. I took off the coat and hung it up again, then unbuckled the holster and put it under the bed, and hoped that no one would come calling that evening.

Who was I kidding? No one had come calling for months.

3

The next day, lunchtime, I got tooled up and went to JJ's for a beer. He was looking a bit green around the gills when I arrived.

'What's up?' I asked.

'I've been thinking . . .' he said.

'Don't,' I interrupted. 'You'll give up everything enjoyable if you start that lark.'

It was quiet again, being mid-week, and by 3.00 pm we were all alone in the bar, just the two of us. I sat where I'd been sitting the previous day, but angled round so that I could view the street through the big window. My mac was open, hanging down and hiding the Howdah.

It was raining again outside. A slow relentless drizzle like a mountain fog. At three-thirty by the Rolling Rock clock on the wall, the Blazer pulled up outside, its wipers beating a slow tick-tock across the windscreen.

'Visitors,' I said.

JJ was polishing glasses again.

The same two geezers piled out of the motor and straight in through the door, put up the CLOSED sign and pulled down the blind. Just like before.

'You still here,' said the black guy to me. 'You're a glutton for punishment, ain't you?'

'He's got no home to go to,' said the white guy.

'Got our money,' said the black guy to JJ.

I slid my left hand inside my coat and pulled the pistol half out of its holster.

11

'No,' replied JJ.

'Cunt,' said the black guy through clenched teeth, and raised his pickaxe handle.

I hauled back the skirt of my coat, pulled the Howdah all the way out of its holster, and pointed it at the black guy's head one-handed. With the other hand I cocked the hammers and felt the two triggers move under my forefinger into firing position. The muzzle was steady, about a foot from his head.

'Put it down,' I said. 'Or you're history. There's a bullet in here will take your head right off. Believe me. Your life depends on it.'

The white guy dropped his bat right away, although I wasn't talking to him. The black guy thought about it, hesitated, then did the same.

'Hands on the bar, both of you,' I said. They obliged.

'Now empty your pockets, and don't fuck about. You first.' I pointed the gun at the white guy. He took out some cash, notes and change, house keys, a driving licence and a used tissue. 'Is that all?' I asked.

He nodded.

'Now you,' I said to the black guy. All he had was a small bundle of bank-notes and the keys to the Chevrolet.

'Count the money,' I said to JJ. He did as he was told. His hands were shaking, but not badly.

'Thirty-eight pounds sixty,' he said. That wouldn't even buy one sleeve of a new Aquascutum.

I picked up the white guy's driving licence. 'Yours?' I asked.

He nodded, too.

'I'm keeping this,' I said. 'You'll have to report it lost. Now I've got your address, so if anything happens here I'll be round with a few mates. Understood?'

He nodded again.

'Stay where you are,' I said to them. To JJ: 'Hold this.' I passed him over the pistol. 'It's a shell, not shot. Aim for

12

the chest. It'll make a hole big enough to drive your car through. And watch it: the fucker kicks like a mule. I'll be right back.' He looked even greener at that.

I bent down and picked up one of the axe handles. I opened the door and went outside to the Blazer. I smashed the windscreen, all the side windows, the back window, both rear-light clusters, the head and spot lights, and the wing mirrors, and snapped off the radio aerial.

A small crowd gathered at the bus-stop to watch, but didn't interfere. The woman from the card shop next to JJ's popped her head out of the door. 'Insurance job,' I said. 'I'm the claims adjuster.' I slung the handle through the broken windscreen and went back into the bar and took the gun from JJ.

'Now fuck off and don't come back,' I said to the two of them. 'You've picked on the wrong people this time. Learn by your mistakes. If I see you round here again, you'll end up in casualty. You, or Mr Lasky. All right?'

Neither of them said anything.

'*All right*?' I asked again.

They both nodded and left, and got into the wreck and drove off with the windscreen-wipers wiping air.

And that's how I got the job of assistant manager at the Twist & Shout.

4

So that was that. I had a job. In a bar. Luxury.

It wasn't hard work. The days were split into early and late shifts. I alternated with JJ, who was restoring a pre-war Harley-Davidson in the lock-up at the back of the bar in his spare time. And, from the bits of oily engine and rusty frame spread around the concrete floor in there, he needed all the spare time he could get.

Early was ten-thirty in the morning to six-thirty in the evening. The bar opened at eleven-thirty, so the first hour was cleaning up after the night before, bottling up, preparing orders and taking in deliveries. Late was six-thirty in the evening until about one the following morning. The bar closed at eleven, except Sundays, just like a regular pub, but it was always murder getting the last of the Billy Bunters out, and then we washed up the glasses and had a final coffee and brandy before shooting off.

It suited me down to the ground. We never heard from the protection boys again, and there was rarely any trouble. The fighters in the area had a couple of pubs to go to where they hosed the blood off the walls every night at closing time, so they didn't bother us much. Besides, I think JJ had told a couple of people about the nasty little toy I'd brought in strapped to my leg that rainy September afternoon, and that helped keep the peace.

JJ's was OK. Friendly, you know. Plenty of people to talk to and newspapers and magazines to read. Good music on the Wurlitzer, good food, good booze, and lots of it.

The rest of the bar staff were young goodlooking women, which didn't hurt one bit, and some of the female clientele would knock your eye out. But apart from being polite, and occasionally getting into a bit of verbal, I mostly ignored them. The feeling was mutual.

The year ended with a three-week-long piss-up over Christmas and the New Year. I suppose I grinned as much as anyone, and wished the customers the compliments of the season, but I didn't enjoy the holidays one bit. I might even have gone a bit heavy at the Grand Marnier from time to time, when it all got too jolly to bear. But no one was counting. No one cared, to tell you the truth.

I could have had Judith down, I suppose. But to see her for a bit and then lose her again would have been worse than not seeing her at all. So I spoke to her on the phone and sent cards and parcels. She sent me two cards back. She pretended one was from my ex-wife, but I knew better, though I didn't say so. And she sent me a great baseball cap. It's all American up in Aberdeen apparently. It was a real quality one, with an adjustable leather strap at the back, and a picture of an oil-rig embroidered on the front. I felt ridiculous wearing it outside, but I'd put it on sometimes when I was in the flat alone. Just so that I felt closer to her. Stupid, I know. I wore it when I ate my Christmas dinner by myself, with just the Queen on the box for company. Not one of my happiest meals. But I survived.

Christmas was followed by the kipper season over January and February, with no one spending much, but we did all right in the bar, even so.

Then winter began to soften into spring as the world turned, until one early morning in March it all came on top again. Just like it always does, sooner or later.

5

I woke up with the beam of a 1000-candlepower torch in my eyes. It was a sudden awakening. The kind they like. The kind that the Nazis, fascists, the secret men have used since time began. Since our ancestors hid in caves and waited for those with the power of life and death to come for them with flaming brands held high against the dark. It was the kind of awakening that robs you of your manhood. Makes you like a child who wants his mother. Undignified. Scary.

I was naked under the sheet and the duvet. I sat up quickly, and was pushed back hard. I raised my arm to shade my eyes from the light, but someone knocked it away. Then a hand appeared. A hand holding a police warrant card, all neat in a leather folder. A big hand, with bitten-down nails and nicotine stains between the first and second fingers. Detective Inspector Chiltern, it read in the spill of the torch's light.

'What do you want?' I said rustily.

'Stay still and shut up,' said a voice. 'Police. We want to talk.'

Police. *Why?* I thought. My conscience was clear. As clear as it was ever going to be.

'What do you want?' I said again.

'We want you. Get up and let's go. Don't mess about.'

'I've got no clothes on,' I said stupidly.

My dirty shirt and jeans landed on the covers in front of me. I sat up and pulled on the shirt. It stank of the bar. I hate that. I swung my legs out of the bed and pulled on my blue jeans. No underwear. But I was glad of anything to cover me: to get back a vestige of dignity.

I stood up to button the fly. The clock on the table next to me said 3.59. Then it moved silently to 4.00. I'd been in bed less than two hours.

I found my shoes and slipped my bare feet into them. I stood there in the beam of the torch and peered beyond it. Into the blackness made even blacker by its light. 'What's the big idea,' I demanded. I was beginning to feel a little braver with some clothes on.

The main light in the room was suddenly switched on, and the power of the beam diminished slightly. There were two average-looking blokes standing looking at me. The one by the light switch was six foot or so, with long greasy yellow hair going a bit thin at the front and pulled into a ponytail at the back. He was wearing a brown leather jacket, jeans and cowboy boots, and looked vaguely familiar. His mate with the torch was shorter, older, with thick brown hair and a week's growth of stubble. He was wearing a similar leather, jeans again, and bumper boots. He was the one with the nail-biting habit.

'Got a warrant?' I said.

Ponytail shrugged. 'Shit no,' he said. 'I knew we forgot something in our enthusiasm to get here.'

'Who are *you*?' I asked.

'Brady. Detective Sergeant,' replied Ponytail.

'No ID?' I said.

'I must have forgotten that too.' He shrugged.

'Take his word for it,' said Chiltern.

I had no choice.

'What do you want?' I asked for the third time. Maybe, some day, one of them would answer me.

'You,' said Chiltern. 'Come on, let's go.'

'Go where?' I said.

'On a magical mystery tour,' said Brady. 'We're off on

the yellow brick road to see the Wizard of Oz.' He giggled and grinned a mad grin, and it occurred to me that there was something badly wrong with him.

'I'm not going anywhere,' I said.

Chiltern sighed. 'Why do people always say that?' he asked no one in particular. 'Listen, Sharman, you're claimed. For the foreseeable future you're the property of the drug squad.'

I looked into Brady's eyes. They stared back as if from another planet. Just what I needed: A couple of undercover cops from the drug squad calling at 4 am. And at least one of them sampling the goods, from the look of him.

'No,' I said.

'Brady,' said Chiltern.

Brady pulled out a set of handcuffs. 'It's this way or the friendly way,' he said. 'Voice your choice.'

The two policemen were both tough-looking individuals. I was well out of condition. Too much booze and rich food. 'All right,' I said. 'But where are we going? I'd like to inform my solicitor.'

'Solicitor. Listen to him,' said Brady. 'You're out of the world, son.' He was at least ten years younger than me. 'Incommunicado. Lost in space. *No* solicitor. You'll be asking for the number of the local Citizen's Advice Bureau next. Now, come on and don't fuck about.'

So I went.

There was a Seven Series BMW parked outside the house, with its sidelights on. I was put in the back along with Brady. Chiltern sat in the front, next to the driver. He was another leather-jacketed character who looked like he worked out a lot.

'Nice wheels,' I said.

'They suffice,' said Chiltern.

'Since when has the Met been laying on motors like this for the squad?' I had a horrible feeling I was being taken for a ride in more ways than one.

Chiltern picked up the thought. 'Don't worry,' he said. 'We're kosher. It's a perk of the job. Drive on, Ollie.'

The driver nodded and started the engine and put on the main beams. He indicated, glanced over his shoulder, and pulled the car into the deserted street.

We headed north through Herne Hill, Camberwell, and the Elephant. I thought that we were going to cross the river, but instead we turned towards Bermondsey. Then into the back streets around London Bridge. The BMW turned into a service road between two buildings, and the reflection of the headlights splashed painfully back into my eyes from a set of mirrored windows. The driver stopped the car in front of a metal door, then pushed a button on a box on top of the dash. The door rattled upward and we drove in.

No one had said a word during the journey. The only sound inside the car had been Joan Armatrading's greatest hits playing at a very low volume on the in-car CD. There was no police radio in the BMW.

The car bumped over the slight hump where the door joined the pavement, and through the entrance and up a ramp. Behind us the shutter rattled down again.

We were in what appeared to be half a warehouse and half a parking garage. There were boxes and cartons piled up the walls, and lots of cars, some covered with dust sheets or tarpaulins and some not. The ones not covered were very upmarket. Mercs, Porsches, more BMWs and even a Rolls-Royce.

'Where the fuck are we?' I asked.

'You'll see,' said Chiltern.

We drove up four storeys and stopped in the middle of an empty floor the size of a football pitch.

'Out you get,' said Chiltern.

'I don't like this,' I said.

'Relax. No one's going to hurt you.'

'Unless you ask for it,' added Brady, and giggled again.

He was beginning to get on my nerves.

I did as I was told. Chiltern and Brady joined me on the concrete floor, and the BMW took off with a long squeal from its fat tyres.

'Over there,' said Chiltern. In the far corner of the warehouse or whatever the hell it was, stood a Portakabin. It was dark and deep in the shadows so that I hadn't noticed it earlier.

We walked over towards it in a flying wedge, me in front. When we got close up, I saw that there was a chink of light under the door. The windows had been blocked off with black paper.

'Inside,' said Chiltern.

I opened the door. It was warm inside the cabin. The heat came from a portable calor-gas stove.

The furniture consisted of a table and four upright chairs, two old armchairs and a filing cabinet. On top of the cabinet was a microwave, an electric kettle, five or six mugs, spoons, and tea and coffee makings.

Sitting at the table, facing the door, was an old acquaintance of mine. Detective Inspector Endesleigh.

He was looking older than when I'd last seen him. Now I'd bet he could get served in a pub without being asked for ID.

His fair hair was longer than I remembered, and he too was dressed in the leather jacket uniform that the other two favoured.

'Sharman,' he said. 'Come in.'

'It's you is it?' I said. 'Why didn't you just call. I'd've come.'

He shrugged. 'I use the phone as little as possible these days,' he said. 'Dogs get sick.'

'You're getting paranoid,' I said.

'So would you if you'd lost two good men in as many weeks.'

'Lost?' I queried. 'You're getting careless aren't you?'

21

Chiltern pushed me from behind. Hard. 'Shut it,' he said. 'It's not funny.'

I looked round. 'OK, OK,' I said. 'Nothing personal.'

'Lost as in dead,' said Endesleigh. 'Sit down and have a cup of tea.'

6

Brady took that as his cue, and went over to put the kettle on. He shook it, then swore under his breath and left the cabin. I heard the sound of running water outside. He came back, plugged in the kettle and pushed the button on the back. He fiddled around with the cups and said to me, 'Coffee or tea?'

'Tea,' I said. 'One sugar, and milk.'

He dropped a tea-bag into a mug, added a spoonful of sugar, picked up a waxed cardboard carton of milk, smelt it, nodded to himself, and splashed some in after the sugar. All the comforts of home, I thought.

We all waited for the kettle to heat up. No one said anything. When it finally boiled and the button clicked out, Brady made the drinks and passed them round.

'Mind if I smoke?' I asked.

'Go on then,' said Endesleigh.

'Anyone got a cigarette?' I asked. 'I came out in a rush. You know how it is.'

Brady took a packet of Marlboro Lights from the pocket of his leather jacket and tossed them to me. I took one.

'Light?' I said.

Brady sighed and found his lighter, came over and fired me up.

'Cheers,' I said. Then I said to Endesleigh, 'What then, Detective Inspector?'

'Detective *Chief* Inspector,' he said back.

23

'Christ!' I said. 'Every time I see you you've put on a rank.'

'That's how I like it,' he said.

'You won't keep on if you lose too many troops,' I told him.

'That's precisely why you're here.'

I didn't like the sound of that one bit. 'And precisely why am I here?' I asked.

'To help us.'

'Don't be stupid,' I said.

'Shut it,' cut in Chiltern.

'Now, Nick,' said Endesleigh. 'Let's be reasonable, shall we?'

'You must be fucking mad if you think I'm going to do anything for you. I'm out of all that lark now. I'm out of everything to do with it – everything I used to be. I work in a bar. I get four pounds fifty an hour, and a meal every session that I do. Occasionally a punter will buy me a beer. Otherwise I buy my own. The only people I know are the customers. I've got no friends away from work. No girlfriend. The last sex I had was a blow job in the ladies after closing, in exchange for a couple of drinks, from some poor bitch who couldn't afford the price of a gin. That was months ago. Lately I think it's for pissing with.'

I didn't know why I was telling them all that.

'My wife's moved to Scotland and taken my daughter. My car needs a re-bore, and sometimes I think I need one myself. I'm living a quiet life. I really don't need you lot to complicate it for me.'

'You're breaking my heart,' said Chiltern. He went over to the filing cabinet, unlocked it with a key from a set he had in his pocket, and pulled open the top drawer. From inside he took out a small cardboard box that he brought over to the table. He took off the lid. From inside it he pulled a pair of disposable plastic gloves and put them on. Then he produced an automatic pistol. He removed the clip and put it back in the box. It was empty. He cleared the breech and placed the gun in front of me. I looked at it gleaming dully in the light. It was a Colt Commander Light Weight. But rather a special one. It had ivory grips with a 'Colt' motif monogrammed on them in gold, The sights were special high profile, and it had ambidextrous safety catches.

'Nice,' I said. 'Special edition?'

He didn't bother to answer. 'Pick it up,' he said.

'Why?'

'Because I say so. Pick it up. You *are* right-handed?'

I nodded.

'In your right hand,' he said.

I did as I was told. It felt good. Smooth in the hand, with no sharp edges.

'Do you know how to dismantle it?' he asked.

I nodded. I'd used one before.

'Do it,' he said.

Again I did as I was told.

When I had the component parts in front of me, he said, 'Put it back together again.'

I did that too.

When I'd finished, he picked it up and put it back in the box. Then he reached in and took out the empty clip, six .45 acp shells and an empty cartridge case: .45 acp again.

'Pick up the case,' he said.

It was just a brass cartridge case. I held it in my hand, then put it back on the table. 'Now load the clip with the rest of the bullets,' he said.

Nothing to it.

He took the clip from me, slid it into the butt of the gun, put the gun and the cartridge case in the box, the box back in the cabinet, and re-locked it.

'Thanks,' he said pleasantly. 'That gun killed one of our team. Whoever did that had cleaned it thoroughly before

25

it was used. Then he wore gloves. There wasn't a print on it. Now there are. *Yours.* All over it. *And* we have the bullet that killed our man.'

'Forensics and ballistics,' I said. 'Inexact sciences both.'

'But combined they could put you away for fifteen years minimum.'

'Come on,' I said. 'That gun's special. Can't you trace ownership?'

Chiltern shook his head. 'It was stolen from a gunsmith in New Cross a year ago. Close to your manor.'

'Jesus Christ! Give me a break,' I said.

He carried on as if he hadn't heard me. 'It was one of a pair,' he said. 'Special order. Consecutive serial numbers. That one's got the lowest number.'

'So I'm a shop-breaker too.'

'You could have bought it in a pub.'

'And what about its mate?'

'Never turned up,' he said.

'Perhaps it will one day.'

'Perhaps it will.'

'And what happens if I have an alibi for the time your man was killed?'

'It was four in the morning. If you're living the kind of quiet life you claim, I'll bet you don't have one,' said Chiltern triumphantly.

'Do you think I'm going to sit still for something like that?' I asked.

'You'll have no fucking choice, son,' he said.

'Endesleigh,' I said, 'are you going to let this happen?'

'What?' He said. 'I don't know what you're talking about.'

'I thought you were straight.'

He shrugged.

I smiled a bitter smile. 'I forgot,' I said. 'No one's straight, are they? Not even the incorruptible Detective *Chief* Inspector Endesleigh.'

'Two dead coppers in two weeks,' he said. 'I'm not losing any more, and I don't care what I have to do to prevent it. You've been sailing close to the wind for years. Now the rent's due. Now you've got to pay or play.'

I took another of Brady's cigarettes from the packet, and he lit it for me. 'I'd like to see you try and make me,' I said.

'I think that can be arranged.'

'How?'

'I don't really think it'll be much of a problem. We have the gun.' He gestured towards the cabinet. 'And your past record. You're a shooter, Nick – and a drug user. It's all in the records. Our man was in the drug squad, and he was shot.'

I stifled a yawn. He didn't like that, I could tell from his expression. 'Motive,' I said. 'I told you I'm leading a quiet life.'

'We can give you a motive,' said Chiltern. 'You decided to earn some serious money. It went wrong.'

'Bollocks. That'll never hang together.'

'Perhaps this will help,' said Endesleigh. He took something out of his jacket pocket and placed it in front of me. It was a bank account passbook. A deposit account. 'Take a look,' he said.

I picked up the book. It was a Middle Eastern bank. The Mayfair branch. Very upmarket. I opened it. The account was in my name. I thumbed through the pages and looked at the entries. They stretched back five years. Regular deposits and withdrawals. Big ones. Very big. At least two a month. For the first time I realised they were serious. Deadly serious. I didn't like it.

'This will never work,' I said. But the words sounded hollow even to me. 'I've never been near this bank.'

'There's staff there will swear you have.'

'I don't believe this.'

'Believe it.'

27

'I'll go higher.'

'Are you going to write to your MP? Or were you thinking of someone in the job? You haven't got a hope. And if you're thinking of appealing to Superintendent Fox, your old mate – don't bother. He's got problems of his own.'

'What kind of problems?'

'You don't want to know. Just take my word for it.'

'And don't think about doing a runner,' said Chiltern. 'We've got this.'

Brady pulled my passport out of his jacket pocket. 'You should be more careful with it,' he said.

'And we know where your daughter is,' said Chiltern.

I went for him then. Straight across the table in a flying tackle which ended up with us both on the floor. Me on top. I managed to get in one good solid whack before Brady kicked me in the kidney and dragged me up by the hair. Chiltern would have finished the job if Endesleigh hadn't said, 'Leave it.'

Chiltern didn't want to. He massaged his jaw where I'd hit him. 'I'll remember that,' he said.

'Do,' I said. 'And threaten my daughter again, and I'll give you plenty more to remember.'

'I said leave it,' said Endesleigh. 'Nobody was threatening your daughter, Nick. He was just letting you know that we know all about you. Now, settle down and be reasonable.'

I didn't have much choice. Brady was stronger than he looked. He put an arm-lock on me and dropped me back in the chair. I didn't say anything, just sat and glowered.

'Well?' said Endesleigh.

I had to go along with them. I didn't have much choice. Not then. Not there. But they couldn't keep me there forever. 'Tell me about it,' I said.

7

Brady made more tea. It was 5.05 by my watch when Endesleigh started. 'There's some extremely nasty people round south London these days,' he said.

Tell me something new, I thought.

'The particular ones I'm referring to sell coke. Some of it goes for crack. Some is sold as plain Charlie. For injecting or smoking or snorting.' As if I didn't know. 'The particular wholesalers we want go to your bar. We know them. *You* must know them. You are going to become good friends. You can regale them with some stories of your past experiences. They'll relate to that. You're going to let them know that you're still involved with people who deal cocaine. We want you to discover exactly what they do – either by accident or because they can't wait to let you know that you're all part of the same great fraternity of scumbags. You, of course, will be amazed. Small world and all that. You'll volunteer to put one party on to the other. Then you're going to make a buy. Ostensibly for your coke-dealing friends. Just a small one at first. To test the water as it were. Then a big one. A very big one. We'll supply the cash for both deals. We'll have details of every note. When the buy's done, we'll nick them. Simple.'

'What about me?'

'You'll be nicked, too.'

'Oh good. Then I'll end up on remand. Probably in the same shovel as the wholesalers. We might even meet when

29

we're slopping out. They can do for me, and you'll have them for murder.'

'It won't come to that,' said Endesleigh. 'You'll get bail. They won't.'

'Yeah? Then their pals come calling one dark night. Just like your pals here did tonight.' I looked at Brady and Chiltern. 'And I'm just as dead. They'll check. They'll find out that you and me know each other . . .' I drew my thumb across my adam's apple in the age-old gesture.

'Don't worry. You'll be safe,' said Endesleigh.

'Oi!' I said. 'Remember me? I used to be in this game. I don't want witness re-location. I'm happy where I am: South London, where all the nasty people live. The chip-on-the-shoulder merchants. I like it here. I fit in. I don't want to end up in Welsh Wales or the bloody Orkneys under a false name.'

'It won't come to that.'

'Sure.'

'Sharman, you were a lousy copper. But you needn't have been.'

'I could have been a contender.'

'Don't be smart. You could have been *the* contender. But no. You lied. You stole. But that wasn't the worst thing. You betrayed your fellow officers. That was the worst thing. You took the piss. You spoiled weeks' worth, even years' worth of honest coppers' work. Because most of us *are* honest. And that's a fact. We do a job against odds that would make most men weep. We just get on with it. Well, it's pay-back time. You owe something, Sharman. And we're the bailiffs. So put up or be banged up. You're well overdue, my son. And from what we can see, there's no one left to miss you. You've finally run out of people to use. What goes round comes round, matey. Now it's our turn to use you.'

'At least you're not appealing to my finer feelings.'

'I didn't think you had any.'

What a charmer, I thought. 'Nice,' I said.

'We're not talking nice. We're talking real.'

'Looks like I don't have much choice.'

'I'm glad you're beginning to see it my way.'

I sat there and smoked another of Brady's cigarettes. My throat was as rough as an emery-board, and my mouth tasted bad. I felt like an animal caught in a trap. I looked around the room, at the three faces. 'And when it's all over, what guarantee do I have that you'll leave me alone in future?' I asked.

'None,' said Endesleigh. 'You'll just have to trust us.'

'Is that supposed to make me feel all warm inside?' I asked.

The three of them just looked at me, and no one said a word.

8

'So who exactly are these people?' I asked.

Endesleigh smiled triumphantly, and took an envelope from his jacket pocket and opened it. He extracted a small stack of Polaroid photographs and dealt them out, one by one, in front of me. I looked at them as he placed them on the table top. Six photos: two men – three photos of each. The first was solid and meaty. He looked tough through a three-day growth of beard. In one photo he stood by a pool, wearing an Hawaiian shirt. In the others he was against an anonymous background wearing a dark suit jacket. I knew him from the bar.

Endesleigh tapped one of the photos of him. 'Patsy Hughes,' he said. 'He's done time for ABH, GBH, armed robbery, obtaining money by menaces. Nice bloke.'

The other geezer looked like a TV presenter, and he knew it. He was young and handsome, with a deep tan and thick dark hair. He was smiling in all of the photos, and showing lots of white teeth. In each he was wearing a white shirt. I knew him too.

Endesleigh tapped one of the photos. 'Roy Seeley. Not the violent type, our Roy. Arrested for living on immoral earnings, fraud, car theft. Never done a minute inside, apart from remand. Do you know them?'

I nodded. 'Not by name, but I've seen them around the bar. The portable phone and Pina Colada mob. Not my types.'

'They will be,' said Endesleigh. 'You're going to learn to love them.'

33

'Sweet,' I said. 'Is that all? I've got an early shift tomorrow. Today,' I corrected myself.

It was his turn to nod.

'Is someone going to give me a lift home?' I asked.

'No,' said Endesleigh, shaking his head.

'Fine,' I said. 'Lend us the money for a cab. I came out without any cash either.'

'No,' he said again.

'What the fuck then?' I was getting well pissed off, and wasn't ready for an early-morning round of Twenty Questions.

'You'll be driving yourself.'

'Do what?'

'You heard.'

'You've brought my car here?' It was late, and I was getting confused.

'No.'

'What, then?'

'You'll see. You're going to like this. Come on.' He stood up and walked over to the door of the cabin. 'Come on,' he said again, more impatiently this time. I stood up and followed him. We crossed the wide empty floor, passed through a set of fire doors, down two flights of stone steps, and through another set of doors on to the next level. Endesleigh turned on the ceiling lights as we went. There were four or five vehicles parked against one wall. They were all shrouded in dust sheets. Endesleigh walked over to one and tugged the sheet free. Underneath was a Ford Sierra.

Big deal, I thought. A fucking rep's car.

Then something about it made me look closer. The paint job was well up to speed. Maroon it was. It gleamed under the lights like a new shoe.

I walked around it. The front bumper swept down almost to the ground, and slightly flared wheel arches covered low-profile tyres on wide Mag wheels. There were airvents in the bonnet and a big spoiler mounted on the boot. Then I saw the discreet badge on the back of the car. *Cosworth 4x4*, it read.

Very good, I thought.

Endesleigh threw me the ignition key. One of those new ones, to fit a high-security lock. I opened the motor up. The interior was upholstered in leather, with Recaro seats at the front. There was a tiny leather steering-wheel, in-car CD, and more switches and digital read-outs than you could decently shake a stick at. I looked inside. The speedometer was calibrated to 170. And that was MPH, not kilometres.

'Shit,' I said. 'Why?'

'Roy Seeley's got one. Black. It's his pride and joy. When he sees this, he's going to talk to you whether you like it or not. They're pretty rare. Just park it outside the bar and Bob's your uncle.'

'Crafty,' I said.

'Don't knock it. The tank's full. It's taxed for a year. The registration, insurance and instruction book's in the glove compartment. There's only three thousand on the clock. It's just run in.'

'You must have been pretty sure of me,' I said.

'We were.'

'It's manual,' I said.

'So?'

'I only drive autos. My foot, you know.'

'You haven't driven one of these. The clutch is as light as a feather. Try it and see. Enjoy.'

'I hope I live long enough.'

'You will. Unless you try and fly this. I believe you can get one-fifty out of it, no sweat.'

'Will you pay my speeding tickets?'

'Sorry. From now on you don't know me. Your contact is Brady.'

'What, that fucking speed freak? If you ask me he's a

couple of gallons short of a full tank.'

'Don't judge a book. Sergeant Brady's not all he seems.'

'I certainly hope not,' I said.

I got in the car and started the engine. It caught right away, and ticked over like a pussy cat. A big pussy cat. I switched on the lights. The dash lit up like the cockpit of Concorde. I reached for the window-winder. Nothing. I looked around and found the button that rolled down the electric window. 'I'll see you, then,' I said.

'Sooner or later. Brady's waiting for you by the main door. Drop him off at home, will you?'

'Sure,' I said. I pushed down the clutch pedal. At least he'd been right about that. It was light. I put the Sierra into first and touched the gas. The purr from the engine turned into a growl. I let the clutch pedal out, and the car rolled gently away. I lifted my hand to Endesleigh, and pointed the nose of the Cosworth towards the ramp heading down.

Brady was leaning against the frame of the big open door downstairs. I drove through and stopped. He pressed a button and ducked under the door as it closed, then ran to the passenger side of the Sierra and got in.

'Don't say we never give you nothin',' he said. 'A Cossie all of your very own. Very nice.'

'I've *got* a car,' I said.

'I thought you said it needed a re-bore.'

'It does.'

'It's an old Jag, isn't it?' he asked.

'Yeah. How do you know?'

'Silly question. We know what colour shorts you wear.'

'That's nice,' I said.

'Junk heap,' he said. I surmised he was talking about my car, not the state of my shorts. 'Give me a Kraut car any day.'

'Like?' I said.

'Porsche 911 Turbo. Now, that is a car.'

'And you've got one?'

'On the firm,' he said.

I shook my head. 'But not tonight.'

'No. Ollie picked me up. We don't want too many cars in and out of here. It might make the local law sus.'

'And we wouldn't want that,' I said.

'No, we wouldn't. This isn't an attachment. We're freelance.' Looking at his eyes in the dawn light, that was what worried me.

'Endesleigh tells me you're my contact.'

'That's right. I'm the mad buyer,' he said. 'Just call me Charlie. My name, my game.' And he giggled again.

'Suit yourself,' I said. But I was still having some doubts. 'Where to, then?'

'Beautiful downtown Kennington. I've got a sweet little drum there. You must come over to dinner sometime.'

'I'll take a raincheck, if you don't mind.'

'Please yourself, babe. It's your loss.'

I drove him to Kennington through empty streets. It took about three minutes. The Cosworth's acceleration was like a kick from a mule. By the time I got to his place I was really motoring, and I didn't mind using a clutch at all.

'Coffee?' he said.

Well, I had to work with the geezer, like it or not. 'Go on then,' I said.

'Remember you're in character.'

'What does that mean?'

'You'll see.'

His house was in a new development, shoehorned between a church and a row of beautiful Georgian houses. One of those private estates built in the eighties, when interest rates were low and mortgages as easy to get as falling off a log. It was an upside-down L-shaped cul-de-sac of smart little terraced red brick boxes, each with its own postage stamp of a front garden and garage, and trailing vines up the walls. His was on the corner, in the angle of the L. He let us in through enough locks to keep a jailer happy.

'Babe!' he shouted as he shut the door behind us. 'I'm home. I'm not alone, so get decent.' He turned and winked at me.

We went through into the kitchen which looked out onto a tiny walled garden, mostly paved, but with two small flower beds and several wooden barrels cut down and full of more flowers.

From somewhere above us I heard movement. Brady put on the kettle. He was good at that.

He took off his jacket and tossed it over one of the kitchen stools. He was wearing a shoulder holster. I could see the butt of a revolver sticking out. It looked like a heavy-calibre weapon.

'You always armed?' I asked.

'Always. You never know what's going to happen, or who you'll meet. I even take it to bed with me. And I'm a good shot. Very good.'

'I'm on your side, remember,' I said.

'Just *you* remember,' he said menacingly, then grinned that maniacal grin again.

Nice bloke, I thought. I'd hate to see the way he treated real villains.

I heard footsteps on the stairs and a young black man, no more than twenty-one, came into the room. He was wearing just a pair of black silk shorts that did nothing to hide a semi-erection. He was bare-chested and muscular, with his hair cut into a high top fade. He stopped at the doorway and struck a pose.

'Who's your friend?' he said in a Geordie accent.

9

Brady didn't turn a hair. Why should he, it was his house.

'Alfie,' he said. 'Meet a friend of mine called Nick. Nick meet Alfie.'

I looked over at Brady, and then at the boy with his dick sticking through the material of his kecks like a flag, and wondered what the hell I'd got myself into this time.

'Hello,' I said.

The black youth ignored me. 'You've been out all night,' he said accusingly to Brady.

'Business,' said Brady back.

'What kind of business?' Alfie looked archly at me.

'Mind your own kind of business,' said Brady, and all of a sudden he wasn't grinning anymore. His face darkened and his eyes gleamed through narrowed lids.

'You could have phoned,' said Alfie. But he'd seen Brady's face, too, and he softened the tone of his voice.

'Who died and made you my keeper?' demanded Brady.

'No one,' said Alfie.

'I phone when I want to phone.' Brady was getting petulant and boring.

'You're always staying out all night with someone,' moaned Alfie.

I didn't quite know what to say. Was this boy accusing me of having it off with Brady, or what? I think he probably was. The whole business was going from bad to worse. 'I'll push off,' I said.

'No,' said Brady. 'Have some breakfast.'

The thought of hot food and liquid, and sharp knives and a gun, and this pair in their present mood didn't do a thing for me.

'No,' I said. 'I need some sleep. I've got work later.'

'I'll catch you at the bar at lunchtime,' said Brady.

Oh, good, I thought. 'I'll look forward to it,' I said.

'What bar?' asked Alfie.

Shut up, Alfie, I thought.

But Brady didn't explode as I thought he might. He just said. 'Where he works.'

'Whereabouts?'

'Norwood,' I said.

'Can I come too?' asked Alfie.

'Another time. It's business,' said Brady.

'See what I mean. It's always bloody business,' complained Alfie. 'I'm going back to bed. You and your friend can do what you like.' And he left.

I looked at Brady. He looked back at me.

'So?' he said.

'So what?'

'I'm glad you said that.'

'Don't keep on,' I said. 'Don't keep pushing. If you're going to be my contact, just be that. If you want to fight, I'm going home. You can keep your fucking car, and do your worst with that bit of trick evidence you fixed up earlier. I told your guv'nor I'm in. Just don't push it. And, by the way, I don't give a shit who you fuck, or what hole you fuck them in, or for that matter if they fuck you. OK?'

'Sure,' he said.

I couldn't resist it. 'But don't the powers that be rather frown on it?' I asked.

'I get special dispensation.'

'Don't you get your leg pulled in the showers?'

'If I do, that's *all* I get pulled, believe me. You were in the job yourself for long enough. Some of those fuckers are so far in the closet they'll never get out. That's how I got started in the clubs and vice squad. No problem with me getting a freebie off a brass.'

I didn't bother mentioning rent boys. 'Listen, I've got to get some kip. What's the time?'

'Half six.'

'Shit, I'm working at ten-thirty. I'm going home. Lunchtime you said?'

'Yeah, we've got to work fast.'

'Those guys don't come in at lunchtime.'

'That's OK. Now, don't forget, when I come in we're close friends.'

'Not *too* close, though.'

'Close enough.'

'You'll get me talked about.'

'Not for the first time, I bet.'

'That's a point. Right, I'm off. I'll see you later.'

'I'll let you out.'

'You believe in security.'

'And you don't. We got into your place last night in twenty seconds flat.'

'I'll get it looked at.'

'I would, if I were you. Seriously.'

And on that happy note I left, and drove home to bed.

10

Of course I was late for work. I'd gone back to bed when I got home, and set the alarm for ten, and then missed it. I woke up with a start at a couple of minutes past eleven. I shaved, washed and dressed in two minutes flat, and hit the road. Normally I walk to work. But that day I took the Ford. As I'd locked up the bar the night before, I had the keys, and when I arrived the cleaner and two draymen with a beer delivery were waiting. 'Sorry,' I said. 'Overslept.' None of them looked particularly impressed. They all had the air of people who had been around since the sun rose, and had nothing but contempt for anyone who couldn't get to work by ten-thirty. I opened up and took in the delivery. The cleaner started swabbing the floor with a damp mop.

'Anything I can do?' I asked.

'Keep out of my way,' the cleaner replied tartly. I left her to it and went out into the kitchen to make some tea.

When the delivery was in, and checked and signed for, and the draymen had drunk a conciliatory bottle of beer each, and the cleaner had cleaned and gone, and the place was ready to open, JJ arrived.

'OK?' he asked.

'Perfect,' I replied.

'Who's the flash motor belong to?' he asked, referring to the Cosworth parked outside on the double yellow lines in front of the bus-stop. Sitting there amongst the usual West Norwood junkers it looked like a thoroughbred in a knacker's yard. It just had *that* look about it, you know.

43

'Me,' I said.

'You?'

'Yeah.'

'You come into money?'

I shrugged.

'That's a thirty-grand motor.'

'Is it?' I said. Which probably wasn't the best thing to say if I was supposed to own the thing.

'Have you sold the E-Type?'

'No.'

'So what's going on?'

'Nothing,' I said.

'Nick . . .'

We were interrupted by the arrival of the first customer of the day. An old boy who wanted a pot of Earl Grey and a croissant with jam. I did the business for him. And then a few more punters started rolling in, and JJ had no chance to question me further.

Brady pulled up outside in his black Porsche, top down, with the stereo blaring BB King, just after one. JJ and I were behind the bar.

'This place is getting like the Royal Automobile Club,' said JJ.

Brady parked opposite, and got out of the car without opening the door. A real athlete. He crossed the street, came in and sat on a bar stool. 'Hi, Nick,' he said.

'I had a hunch you'd know him,' said JJ.

'Hi, Brady,' I said. 'What'll you have?'

'Give me a beer and a burger. Medium rare with French fries. No onion in the salad.'

I got the beer, and JJ took the food order through to the kitchen.

'So what's up, Nick?' asked Brady.

'Not a lot. I was late for work, thanks to you.'

'This is not the Nick Sharman I heard about. Working in a dump like this for a few quid an hour, and worrying

44

about being late. That sounds like a normal citizen.'

'It suits me.'

'You must be losing your touch.'

'Brady, why don't you back off. I told you those two guys don't come in here during the day. If they come in at all, it's Friday or Saturday evening. Now you've seen me at work, so just get lost.'

'I've seen you at work before, Nick. This isn't the first time I've been here.' Now I knew why he looked familiar. 'I believe in knowing the territory,' he went on.

'Good for you.'

'Do you think they'll be in tonight?' he asked.

'God knows. It's Friday. Maybe.'

'And?'

'And I finish at six-thirty. I'll stick around. I'm not working 'til tomorrow evening. I'll see what's cooking.'

'My burger would be good.'

'Be patient, Brady. Everything comes to him who waits.'

He took a sip of his beer. 'I have waited,' he said. 'Too long. I want these people. Through them we can get the importers. The fat cats sitting in their offices in the city. The ones with all the money, who never get their hands dirty on the stuff. I want those bastards, Nicky my boy, and I want them bad.'

The bell in the kitchen rang. 'This'll be yours now,' I said.

'Well run along and get it then, like a good waiter.'

'I could learn to dislike you,' I said. 'Easily.'

He twisted up his face in a leer. 'I think you're getting me confused with someone that might worry about it,' he said.

I shrugged and went and got his food. JJ grabbed my arm as I picked up the plate. 'You do know him,' he said.

'Slightly,' I replied.

'Watch him, mate. He's bad news.'

You don't know the half of it, I thought. 'He's harmless,' I said.

JJ didn't look convinced. Nor did I, to tell you the truth.

11

Brady took the hint. He ate his burger and drank his beer
and left. Being Friday lunchtime, it was busy in the bar
and I didn't have time for conversation anyway. Good job.
All afternoon I felt JJ watching me, but he didn't say
anything. At six-thirty when the two barmaids who were
doing the evening shift turned up, I took off my apron and
sat at the bar.

'Not going?' asked JJ.

'No, I've got tomorrow off. I think I'll stick around for
a bit.'

'I would have thought you'd've had enough of this
place for one day.'

'No,' I said. 'You know I love it. Give us a beer, for
God's sake. I'm spitting feathers here.'

'You're driving, don't forget,' he said, giving me a
bottle of Rolling Rock.

'It's got right up your nose, that motor, hasn't it?' I
said.

'No.'

'Yes, it has. What's the problem?'

'How can you afford it?'

'What. On what you pay me, you mean?'

'Yeah, if you must know.'

'You know I've got a little dough put away. Relax, for
Christ's sake.'

'And what about that geezer?'

'Who?'

'Who? You know very well. Him in the Porsche.'

'What about him?'

'Where does he fit in?'

'He doesn't. He's a customer. He's been in before.'

'Not talking to *you*, he hasn't.'

'So he's talking to me now. Things change. What about it?'

'He smells bad.'

'I'll get him some aftershave for Christmas.'

'Don't get funny, Nick.'

'I don't understand what the problem is.'

'Just don't bring trouble here.'

'The last time there was trouble here, you were pleased to see me.'

'Those two were nothing. That guy's different.'

'No trouble, JJ, I promise. All right?'

'All right,' he said. But it was grudging.

I stayed around, dawdling over two beers until about nine. I chatted to the staff and a couple of customers, and it was really no hardship. Then about ten past, Hughes and Seeley came by. I saw them outside. As they passed the Ford, Seeley grabbed Hughes by the sleeve, and they stopped and gave it a good screw. I pretended not to notice. Then they came in and went up to the other end of the bar and ordered a couple of beers. Then Seeley called JJ over. I saw JJ point at me, and a minute or two later they moved in my direction. They were dressed for their summer holidays or a winter cruise. Baggy lightweight suits. Seeley's was beige, Hughes's olive green. Both wore button-down cotton shirts: the kind that looked like they'd never seen an iron, you know. Tan for Seeley, white for Hughes, teamed with colourful ties. On their feet were light loafers, like boat shoes. I guessed these two went shopping together. Hughes was carrying a small portable phone. I knew one of them would have to.

'Your motor?' said Seeley, pointing at the Cosworth

parked outside. He had a London accent. Not cockney, just anonymous London.

'Yeah,' I said.

'Nice,' he said.

'Yeah,' I said again.

'Had it long?'

'No.'

The other one, Hughes, just stood there looking at me. I hadn't liked them before, and being close didn't make things better. 'I've got one too,' said Seeley.

'That's nice.'

'What made you get one?'

'They're fast, and anonymous, and they piss off fuckers in BMWs,' I said.

He laughed at that, and showed his mouthful of white teeth just like in the photos I'd seen. 'That's right,' he said. 'Want a drink?'

I didn't, but I'd told Endesleigh I was in, so I grinned back. 'Lovely,' I said. 'A Rock'll do.'

Seeley ordered three, and we all introduced ourselves, although I already knew who everybody was.

'You work here don't you?' said Hughes, speaking for the first time. His voice was surprisingly cultured for someone who looked so rough.

'Yeah,' I said.

'You must have a private income to have a motor like that.'

It's funny how everyone was getting interested in the state of my finances all of a sudden.

'Something like that,' I said. 'I couldn't afford it on what I earn here, that's for sure.'

'Come into money, have you?'

'Not really. I do bit of this and that on the side.'

'Like?'

'It's none of your business, Pat,' said Seeley, but real friendly like, so no one could possibly take offence.

'That's all right,' I said. 'No worries. It's not a secret. Anything that comes up, you know.' I could be coy with the best of them.

They knew all right.

'So what do you two do?' I asked.

'The same,' said Hughes. 'This and that.'

They were being coy, too.

We drank our beer, and chatted about cars and clothes and women, like real men do, until just after ten Seeley said, 'What you doing later?'

'Going home to bed,' I said. 'I didn't get much kip last night, and I've been working all day. I'm knackered.'

'Want to come out, have a laugh?'

'Not tonight,' I said. 'I'm fucked.'

'We've got something that'll wake you up.' He touched his nose and winked.

I knew I might never get another chance so easy. 'Is that right?' I said.

Seeley grinned and nodded. I said goodbye to my bed for another night.

'All right, you're on,' I said.

'We'll do some in the motor,' said Hughes.

'Do we need two cars?' I said.

'Where do you live?' asked Seeley.

'Local. Just round the corner.'

'No, you're all right. I'm close by. We'll go in mine. I'll drop you off after.'

'Come round my place, then,' I said. 'I'll have to change. I feel like a right scruff next to you two.'

'Sounds good,' said Seeley.

So we all left. JJ gave me a dirty look as we went, but I couldn't help all that.

12

Their car was parked about a hundred yards down the street. I watched them walk towards it, then got into mine, started it, indicated, pulled out, and flashed them as I went past. I looked in the mirror and saw them pull out behind me, and I kept going slowly until they caught up. I took it easy on the short run to my place. I parked at the kerb outside, and the black Cosworth slid to a halt behind me. I got out and walked back to their car.

'In there,' I said, pointing at the house when they joined me on the pavement.

Hughes looked at my Jag parked up in front. 'Whose is that?' he asked.

'Mine,' I said.

'How many cars have you got, for Christ's sake?'

'Just the two.'

I think he was impressed, and I enjoyed that.

We all went inside, and up to my flat. 'I'm going to take a quick shower,' I said.

'Got a mirror?' asked Seeley. I went into the bathroom and hauled my shaving mirror off the wall, wiped it off with a towel, and took it out to him. I grabbed the strides from a dark blue suit, a shirt, some clean socks and shorts, and dived back for a quick splash. I towelled down and put on the clothes and went back into the living-room. I wondered if they'd gone through my stuff in my absence. I didn't care. There was nothing for them to find.

When I got back, Seeley had cut out three lines, each as

51

thick as my little finger, on the mirror. I was going to have to go for it whether I liked it or not.

'You didn't waste much time,' said Hughes.

'Didn't want to miss out on the goodies,' I said.

'Spoken like a real junkie,' said Seeley, rolling up a new fifty into a tube.

I watched them scarf up a line each, then I took my turn. It was primo gear. I felt the familiar rush, and tasted metal at the back of my throat. 'Good stuff,' I said.

'Only the best for friends of ours,' said Seeley.

'Thanks,' I said. 'I'll remember that.'

I went and chose a tie equally as colourful as the ones they were wearing, and knotted it, then tugged on my suit jacket, slipped my feet into a pair of soft, black leather loafers, fetched my wallet from the bathroom, and I was ready.

'OK, then,' I said. 'Let's go if we're going.'

'Where do you fancy, Pat?' asked Seeley as we went downstairs.

'There's only one place to go when we're carrying,' said Hughes.

'Sonny's?' asked Seeley.

'In one.'

'Where's that?' I said.

'You've never been to Sonny's?' said Seeley. 'You've never lived.'

'Then I haven't lived. So where is it?' I asked again.

'Round the back of Beak Street. You're going to like it there.'

We drove up to town in Seeley's Cosworth. Inside, it was the twin of mine, black leather and all. He was proud of his driving, you could tell, but he drove too close, and at every set of lights he ended up in the wrong lane. I didn't say anything.

Sonny's was the kind of place I didn't think existed anymore

— I don't know why, I just didn't. It was in an old crooked house squeezed in between two modern office buildings in a street off Beak Street. The place was quiet when we arrived, with the windows curtained tightly. There was no name-plate or sign to indicate that there was anything unusual inside, just a plain black painted wooden door at the top of three whitewashed stone steps. Seeley rang the doorbell. When an almost invisible shutter opened, I half expected him to say, 'Joe sent me.' He didn't. He said nothing, but the door opened immediately.

Inside was an entrance hall decorated with the same flock wallpaper that they had in my local Indian restaurant. The door had been opened by a big geezer in a tuxedo, who accepted Seeley's fiver tip like it was his right, and said, 'You know the way, gents.'

Seeley and Hughes obviously did. I just followed, still buzzing from the coke, along the hall, down two steps, and we were there.

The club itself had been formed by knocking through all the rooms on the ground floor. There was more flock wallpaper, a dark red carpet, Burgundy leather furniture, a small stage, and a dark wooden bar along one wall. George Shearing was playing 'Honeysuckle Rose' softly through the speakers at each side of the stage, and draped across a lot of the furniture were the real attraction of the place. Half a dozen or so women ranging in age from their teens to their early thirties, in various stages of undress. As we entered the room they recognised Hughes and Seeley, and we were suddenly surrounded by a crowd of the friendliest whores I've ever seen, all saying hello and rubbing themselves up against our heroes like they'd just liberated Soho from the German army.

One of the girls, a big blonde cruelly corseted in a black basque with a leather micro-skirt and black fish- nets on a pair of legs that seemed to go on forever and a day, said, 'Who's your friend, Roy?' Giving me the once over like I was a fish on a slab.

'This is Nick,' said Seeley. 'You want to take care of him, Kylie?'

'If you'll take care of me first,' she said with a flutter of false eyelashes.

'Get behind the bar and get us all a drink and I'll see what I can do,' he said.

'What'll it be?' asked Kylie.

'The usual, please, darlin'. We've had a good week. We're celebrating. And give us a dry cloth while you're there, there's a love.'

He took a plastic baggie of coke from his jacket pocket. There was enough to get a coach party high – and then some. Just as well, I thought, as I saw the girls' eyes light up at the sight of it. The blonde did as she was told, and went behind the bar and handed Seeley a folded Irish-linen glass cloth, then lined up enough champagne glasses for everyone, took three bottles of Moët from the fridge at the back, and expertly removed the corks without flooding the place. She filled the glasses, and everyone helped themselves.

Meanwhile Seeley wiped the bar top with the cloth to make sure it was dry, then poured out a pile of charlie from the bag, and crushed down the rocks with the edge of a credit card, and pulled out a line about a yard long across the polished surface. Then the trusty fifty came out again.

'There you go Steph,' he said, and handed it to a dark girl in a red mini-skirt and a red see-through blouse which made her breasts look like they were covered in blood, and which turned her nipples the colour of raspberries, and she hoovered about six inches off the line up her nose.

'Me next,' insisted Kylie, and she took the note from Steph and bent down to snort up her share, and showed a cleavage deep enough to lose your car keys in. She took her hit, and stood back and said, 'Champagne and coke make me *so* horny.' And gave me a look that could have blistered paint, and dived into her champagne again.

'You've had a result, mate,' said Ray. 'That Kylie's a great fuck. Believe me, I know.'

Terrific, I thought. The *Good Housekeeping* Seal of Approval. That's all I need.

We all took our turns at snorting the coke. Afterwards I grabbed Seeley and said, 'What's this place all about, then?'

'It's all about tarts, mate. What does it look like?'

'Are we the only ones here?'

'It's early yet. It doesn't really get going 'til one or two in the morning. Then it'll be buzzing, you'll see. Are you going off with Kylie, or what?'

'I don't know yet. What's the deal?'

'They've got rooms upstairs. It ain't the Ritz, but it does.'

'How much?' I asked.

'If you've got to ask, you can't afford.'

'Bollocks, Roy,' I said. 'How much?'

'A couple of hundred, two-fifty. But it's worth it, believe me. Especially with her.'

'I'll think about it.'

'Don't think about it too long. She's a popular girl. I'd go case with her myself, but I fancy that Steph something strong. Anyway, don't worry about money. Just have a good time.'

'I'm not worried about the money,' I said. I wasn't. I just wanted to know the score. Old habits die hard.

I took a sip from my glass and lit a cigarette.

Kylie came out from behind the bar and joined us.

'Got one for me?' she asked.

'I'll just bet he has,' said Seeley with a leer.

'I meant a cigarette, Roy.'

'Course you did, sweetheart. Only joking. Now I'm going to leave you two alone to get acquainted while I go and have a word with Steph.'

'Go on, then,' said Kylie. 'I want to find out all about your friend Nick.'

'See you then,' said Seeley, and took his glass, and made tracks for the girl with the red see-through blouse.

'I meant it, you know,' said Kylie. 'I do want to know everything about you.'

'No you don't,' I said.

'You'd be surprised.'

'No, I wouldn't.'

'Don't you like me?'

'Sure I do.'

'Then let's have another drink.' She stretched over and hooked an open bottle of champagne. As she did so her leather skirt stretched tightly over her buttocks. One up to Kylie. She knew exactly what she was doing. She topped up my glass, and then hers. 'Cheers,' she said.

'Cheers,' I replied, and we touched glasses. She looked at me over the rim of hers as she drank. A long bedroom look through wide, cornflower-blue eyes. She stroked her other hand slowly down her body from breast to thigh, feeling every curve, and licked her lips.

'You remember what I said about coke and champagne?' she said.

'I remember.'

'It was true, every word of it.'

'I guessed it was.'

'And now I've had both.'

'So you have.'

'And now I've got an itch in my cunt that needs scratching.'

'Any candidate for the scratcher,' I asked.

'Yes,' she said. 'You. You look like you might be good at it.'

'I'm flattered.'

'I bet you could scratch me raw.'

'I could try.'

'Come on, then.'

'What, *now*?'

'Yes.'

'I hate to break up the party.'

'It'll still be going on when we get back.'

'OK, let's go then,' I said.

So we did.

I grabbed the champagne bottle, and Kylie took our glasses and her handbag from where she'd been sitting and we made for the exit. On the way I caught Seeley's eye and held up the bottle and pointed at it. He gave me a letter O with the thumb and forefinger of his left hand. I flipped him a wave of thanks, then Kylie and I went out into the front hall, through a door halfway along, then up two flights of steep, narrow stairs, along a dimly-lit corridor, until Kylie opened a door on our left, leaned in, and switched on a light.

'Come on in,' she said. 'Be it ever so humble . . .'

13

The room was small and very clean. It was lit by two wall-mounted fixtures covered with tiny lampshades. The walls were decorated with plain beige paper, dotted with framed sporting prints that someone obviously thought gave the place a touch of class. Someone had been wrong.

The floor was covered with a dark brown carpet, and matching dark brown curtains were drawn tightly across the windows. There was a hand-basin against one wall, with a fresh cake of soap on top of a pile of folded flannels behind one tap, and a white towel draped across the front of it. Above the basin was a mirror about two foot square, with a shaving plug next to it, and a short, opaque, unlit fluorescent tube above the mirror. On the carpet underneath stood a metal waste-bin.

The bed was a threequarter double covered with just a white sheet, and two pillows at the head. On one side of it was a small table with a glass ashtray centred on it, on the other a single straight-backed chair with a thin duvet in a flowered cover folded on it. Against the wall opposite was a dark brown corduroy-covered armchair. I put the champagne bottle on the bedside table and Kylie placed the glasses and her handbag next to it. I sat on the edge of the bed and felt a rubber sheet through the thin white cotton. All in all it was like any cheap room in any plastic hotel in any city in the world.

'Nice, isn't it?' said Kylie.

I looked over at her and she winked and pulled a face.

'You don't really live here, do you?' I asked.

'Are you kidding? I've got a lovely flat in Brewer Street.'

'A bit noisy down there, isn't it?'

'Double-glazed.'

'I'm impressed.'

'You're making me sound like an estate agent.' She stood in the centre of the room and smiled at me. 'So what are we waiting for?'

'How much is this all going to set me back?' I asked.

'What does it matter?'

'It matters.'

'I wouldn't worry about it. Roy always picks up the tab for his friends.'

'Does he?' I said.

'Yes,' she replied. 'He's a generous bloke. This is his champagne, remember.' She picked up the bottle and held it up to the light. 'That'll do,' she said and filled our glasses, and gave one to me. She went over and peered in the mirror. I saw her pull another face into it, like she didn't like what she saw. She looked OK to me. 'I wish we had some more coke,' she said. 'Oh, hell, not to worry.' And she drained her glass and put it in the sink.

She came and sat next to me, kicked off her shoes and pulled up her skirt, and undid the suspenders that held up her stockings. She was wearing a musky perfume, and the heat from her body radiated the smell of it until it seemed to fill my head. She rolled down her stockings, pulled them off, then dropped them on the floor. She leant over and kissed me. Her tongue filled my mouth and she bit my lip. I watched as she stood up again and undid her skirt and let it fall to the floor and stepped out of it. The basque she was wearing ended just below the swell of her hips. With it she had on only a tiny black lace G-string which hardly covered the mound of her blonde pubic hair. She struck a model's pose then turned around.

'Unhook me,' she said.

The corset was fastened with about thirty hooks and eyes, and it was so tight it was hard to get a purchase on the slippery elasticated material at the back.

I finally got it undone and she shrugged out of it, and tossed it on to the armchair and turned and came into my arms. She was soft and hot, and I stroked my hand down her back and she shivered and rubbed her crotch into the top of my thigh, so that I could feel the pubic bone.

'That feels good,' she said.

'I'm glad you like it,' I said back, and stroked her some more.

'Nick,' she said.

'What?'

'I've been a very bad girl,' she said.

'Is that right?'

'Yes, I need punishment.'

'Do you?'

'Yes, I deserve a good spanking.'

I pulled her away from me and looked at her. She lowered her eyes demurely.

'So that's what you're into,' I said.

She nodded. 'Have you done it before?'

'Of course.'

'So you must like bad girls.'

'I do.'

'I thought you would.'

'Will you tie me up?' she asked.

'Sure. What with?'

'My stockings.'

'OK.'

'Tie me up and gag me and beat my bottom until I come,' she said. I could feel her trembling, and smell her woman's smell under the musk of perfume.

I did what she wanted. I tied her wrists tightly with one of her stockings, and gagged her with the other. As soon as I started she begged me to stop, but I knew she didn't want me to. And, besides, I was starting to get into it. I left her tiny panties on; somehow she looked almost more naked wearing them.

By the time I'd forced the stocking into her mouth and knotted it behind her head she was writhing on the bed like she was really scared, and I pulled her across my knee and started spanking her. She was all over the place trying to get away, but I wouldn't let her. She was moaning and growling through the gag, and I could hardly hold her she was so strong.

Then all of a sudden she climaxed with a muffled scream and a spasm, and lay still across me. I rolled her over and pulled the gag loose. It was soaked with spit.

'Oh Christ, Nick, that was fucking wonderful,' she said breathlessly. 'Got a cigarette?' She was sweating, and her make-up had run. She looked as sexy as hell, and she knew it.

I untied her hands and found my Silk Cut and gave her one and lit it, and one for myself, and dropped the match into the ashtray. I lay back on the bed next to her and she snuggled up close to me.

'God, I love being beaten,' she said. 'Do you think that's weird?'

'Whatever turns you on,' I said.

'What do you like?' she asked.

'Just about anything.'

'I just bet you do. You're a bit of a naughty boy yourself, aren't you?'

'Sometimes.'

She wriggled about to get comfortable. 'My arse is burning,' she said. 'I've got to come again.'

'You will,' I said.

'I believe you.' She reached over for the champagne bottle and drank straight from the neck. 'Want some?' she asked.

'Sure,' I said. I took it and did the same. It was getting warm, but it tasted good.

'Do you mind me being a whore?' she asked.

'Why should I mind?'

'Some men do.'

'I don't. I used to have a girlfriend who was on the game.'

'You're full of surprises. Didn't you care?'

'No,' I said. 'She did what she did, and I did what I did.'

'Which was what?'

'I used to be a copper.'

She stiffened, and I felt her move back and study me through mascara-streaked eyes.

'Don't worry,' I said. 'They kicked me out.'

'What for?'

'Stealing,' I said.

'I said you were a naughty boy.'

'Yes, I was.' I was serious, but she thought I was kidding. That was OK. It went with the geezers I'd come in with.

'What did you steal?'

'Dope.'

'What kind?'

'What we were doing tonight. I used to be a heavy user.'

'You still must be, if you're in with those two.'

'I only met them tonight.'

'You're honoured – being brought here.'

'Maybe.'

'I mean it.'

She stubbed out her cigarette and took mine from between my fingers and did the same with it. 'Take your clothes off,' she said. 'You're on a promise remember.'

'I remember.'

'And don't do anything. It's *your* turn now. But I'll have to put a condom on you. Sorry.'

'I understand.'

'And wash you, although that's a load of bollocks really.'

Literally, I thought, but didn't say anything. She got up and went to the sink, filled it with water, and wet and soaped a flannel. Then came back and washed me, and dried me with the towel from the sink. She was very gentle, and got me more than interested.

'God, but you're big, Nick,' she said.

I had to laugh. 'I bet you say that to all the boys,' I said.

'I do, but in your case it's true.'

'I bet you say that to all the boys, too.'

'You'd lose your bet.'

'Kylie, you're a bloody liar.'

'Sshh,' she said, and went down on me. She knew exactly what to do. A real expert. Everytime I got close to climax, she squeezed my balls tightly.

'You're driving me crazy,' I said. 'I can't stand much more.'

'Wait.' She took a condom out of her handbag, undid the foil, and expertly fitted it on me. Then she rolled over and lay with her legs open, and pulled the G-string to one side. 'Come in me,' she whispered.

I did as I was told.

She pulled me down close and whispered. 'Fuck me, Nick. Fuck me hard. Batter me, you bastard. Come on.'

I did as I was told again. I fucked her as hard as I could, and she loved it. She entwined her arms and legs around me, pulling me tightly into her body, and we found a rhythm that excluded everything in the world until I felt like a bottle with its cork about to explode, and she knew and, as I came, she came with me, and as she did she screamed my name in my ear.

We collapsed into a sweaty tangle of limbs and lay still, breathing hard. She leant up on one elbow and put her mouth so close to my ear I could feel her breath inside my head. 'That was great sweetheart,' she said. 'The best. And I swear I don't say that to any of the boys. Now, have a sleep and I'll take care of you.' And she reached over and pulled the duvet off the chair and tugged it over us.

14

I don't know how long we lay there for. Maybe half an hour, maybe longer. I was half asleep, half drunk, and half speeding like a car in neutral with the accelerator pedal hard on the floor. Then Kylie got up, prepared another warm flannel, disposed of the condom, and gently washed me again. 'After-sales service?' I said.

'That's right.' When she'd finished, she said, 'I've got to go to the loo. Can I borrow your shirt?'

'Sure.'

She put it on, and picked up her handbag and went to the door. 'I won't be a minute,' she said, and blew me a kiss.

I sat up and lit another cigarette. It tasted lousy. I was getting a headache and my mouth was dry. I picked up the champagne bottle and shook it. Empty. I swung my legs over the side of the bed and put on my socks and shorts. I got up and pulled on my trousers and put on my shoes. I went to the window and pulled back the curtain. The room I was in was at the back of the house. It was surrounded by dark office blocks, but the sky was red with reflected light from the city. I stood there looking into the blackness until Kylie came back. She'd washed her face and put on fresh make-up. She took off my shirt and picked up her basque from where she'd thrown it.

'Do me up, will you?' she asked. I did up the hooks at the back and she produced a fresh pair of stockings and a clean G-string from her handbag and bundled up the dirty ones and pushed them to the bottom of it. 'You don't mind all this, do you?' she asked. 'You can go back downstairs if you want to.'

'I don't mind,' I said.

'Good. I hate men who fuck and run.'

I had to laugh. I picked up my shirt from the bed where she'd dropped it, and put it on whilst she finished dressing. It smelt of her perfume and her sex. 'Got a comb?' I asked.

'A brush.'

'That'll do.'

She took a hairbrush from her handbag and gave it to me. There was a lot of blonde hair caught up in the bristles. I went over to the mirror and brushed my hair back into shape. Then re-tied my tie and put on my jacket. She checked herself in the mirror too and, once satisfied, we were both ready.

'Let's go see how the party's doing,' she said.

We went downstairs, where the music on the speakers was louder and faster. When we got into the club it was much busier than when we'd left. There was an older, brassier woman behind the bar, there seemed to be more girls around, and half a dozen men in suits were drinking at the bar or talking to the girls.

'Business is booming,' I said.

'It's quiet tonight,' said Kylie, waving hello to a couple of the punters. 'Stay here. I won't be a minute. I want to speak to Lily.' She went up to the woman behind the bar and said something. A short conversation ensued and then she came back and joined me. 'Just adding myself to the bill,' she said. 'Your friends are upstairs. They asked you to wait. They won't be long.'

'Do you want a drink?' I asked.

'Sure.'

'Champagne?'

'Of course.'

We went over to the bar together. 'A bottle of Moët,' I said to the woman.

'Yes, dear,' she replied.

'Lily, this is Nick,' said Kylie. 'He's with Roy and Pat.'

'Oh, yes,' said Lily. 'Roy told me to put everything on his bill. One bottle of Moët coming up.'

'*Everything*?' I asked.

'Yes, love. Everything your heart desires is what he said.' She produced a bottle of champagne and two glasses.

'Give me a beer, Lily,' I said. 'This stuff's too rich for my blood.'

'Heineken or Beck's, dear?' asked Lily.

'Beck's'll do,' I said.

She went back to the fridge and got me a bottle. She put it and a glass on the bar in front of me. Meanwhile Kylie was soaking up the champagne like raindrops on a hot pavement.

'Do you work here every night?' I asked her when Lily went off to serve another customer.

'No. Why?' she asked innocently. As if she didn't know.

'Just interested. Are you involved with anyone at the moment?'

'No. I'm free white and single. Why?' All innocence again. But she couldn't keep from smiling.

'The same. Just interested. I thought I might be round Brewer Street one evening soon, and I could buy you a meal. There's some very good restaurants round there.'

'That's true.'

'So?'

'What?' She wasn't even trying to hide her amusement by then.

'You know what.'

'Mixing business and pleasure can be fatal,' she said.

'It's the same with smoking and drinking and fucking, or so they tell me.'

69

She smiled. 'I'm free Wednesday,' she said.

'Me too,' I said. I didn't know if I was, but I would be.

'What a coincidence,' she said.

'Isn't it? So what do you say?'

'OK, Nick. Wednesday then. Do you know a pub called The Sun And Seven Cantons?'

'Sure I do. It's just round the corner isn't it?'

'Great Pulteney Street. Meet me in there at eight.'

'Don't you want me to call for you?'

'No. You're a punter, Nick. A very nice punter, I won't deny. But still a punter, and I don't give punters my address.'

'Or phone number?'

'No. Let's take it easy. If I get to like you, you'll get it all.'

'Don't you like me now?'

'Yes, I do. That's the trouble. I *never* date guys from here. That's my rule. I'm making a big exception with you.'

'Will you change your mind?'

'No.'

'Shall I give you my number, just in case?'

'Good idea. Something might crop up, and I don't want you to have a wasted journey.' She took a small address book from her bag and found the 'N' page. 'Nick what?' she asked.

'Sharman,' I replied.

I gave her my home number and the number of the bar. 'You work in a bar?' she said. 'The last thing I'd've taken you for was a barman.'

'It's a long story,' I said.

'Tell me on Wednesday. I do want to know about you – I wasn't lying.'

'I thought that was just a line.'

'It is. But sometimes even a line can be the truth. Hey, here's your friends back.'

15

I looked round, and Seeley and Hughes were coming back through the door. Seeley was with Steph, and Hughes was with a girl who looked like she might get to the age of consent within a year or two. All four of them came over to us.

'All right, Nick?' asked Seeley, who seemed to be in high good humour, and totally out of his mind.

'Fine.'

'Good.'

'You?'

'Never better. Me and Pat have been taking advantage of the amenities.'

'That's nice,' I said.

'You too, eh?'

'Yeah.'

'Enjoy yourself?'

'Yeah.' I looked over at Kylie and she winked.

'Not letting on, eh?' he said. 'I like that. A man of few words.'

I nodded.

'That's good. I like a bloke who can keep his gob shut. I see you've got some more booze in. I'm ready for another myself. Lil,' he called, 'a couple more bottles of bubbly over here.'

'Right, Roy,' she answered. She brought out another pair of dark green champagne bottles and four more glasses, and filled them all up.

'So, Nick,' said Seeley when he'd three-quarters emptied his, 'what do you think of the old place?'

'Top of the shop,' I said.

'I know a couple of places like this, but Sonny's is the best. Best girls in London, eh, Steph?'

'That's right, Roy,' Steph agreed. The state she was in she would have agreed to anything. And probably already had done.

'So what are we doing?' asked Hughes.

Seeley looked at his watch. 'I'll have to be off soon. You know how it is?'

'I know,' said Hughes. 'What about you, Nick?'

'Me too,' I said. 'I'm working tomorrow.'

'Jesus! What a pair,' said Hughes.

'You want a lift, don't you?' Seeley said to me.

'If you're going my way.'

'I've got to get back to Dulwich. I'll drop you off. Pat, what about you?'

'I'm not under the cosh like you,' said Hughes. 'I'll catch a cab later.'

'You going to settle up, then?'

'Course.'

'I owe you . . .' I said, reaching for my wallet. 'Keep your money, Nick,' said Seeley. 'It's on us tonight. You can pay next time. I said we'd had a good week. Pat'll take care of everything.'

'You sure?' I said. 'I don't want to ponce off you.'

'Sure I'm sure. Like I said, next time it's your shout.'

'All right, then,' I said. 'Thanks. It's been a good night.' Then to Kylie, 'Looks like I'm off.'

'Take care,' she said.

'I'll see you again.' She knew what I meant.

'Sure you will.'

Seeley tapped me on the arm. 'Come on, Nick. Leave her alone. Let's go if we're going.'

I said good-night all round and we left. On the way

back to Tulse Hill, Seeley's driving was even worse than it had been earlier. We were lucky not to get a pull. He dropped me off outside my place just after three.

16

I went straight to bed when I got in, but I couldn't sleep at first. Too much coke in my system. I just lay in bed and dozed. I finally fell asleep properly around eight, and didn't wake up until noon. I got up and went out to get a paper and some milk. When I got back, Brady's Porsche was parked behind the Cosworth. He was leaning against his car waiting for me.

'Oversleep?' he asked.

'Late night.'

'Sonny's?'

'How the hell do you know?'

'I know everything. Can we go inside? I fancy a coffee.'

We went up to my flat and I put the kettle on. 'Black or white?' I asked.

'White. One sugar.'

I made him a coffee, and tea for myself. 'Am I being followed?' I asked.

'That's right. I must say you didn't waste any time getting to know our boys. I like that.'

'They got to know me. The car worked just like Endesleigh said it would.'

'Shrewd bloke. Youngest DCI in the country.'

'Is that right?'

'It is. So, how was Sonny's?'

'Interesting.'

'You get fucked?'

I nodded.

'Which one?'

'Kylie.'

'Oh, Kylie. Hot stuff I believe.'

'You know her, too?'

'Course I do. I know all the tarts who work there. I told you I like to know the territory.'

'Bit of a waste for you, isn't it?'

'Don't get funny.'

'Sorry.'

'So what's the strength with Seeley and Hughes?'

'We're going out again. It could get pricey. I'll need some exes. I am supposed to be a bit of a ducker and diver, after all. Break into the contingency fund.'

'I'll see what I can do. How much?'

'Well, last night's little caper must have cost the best part of a grand. They paid for everything.'

'Including Kylie?'

I nodded.

'You did have a result. And you want exes money as well. What were you drinking?'

'Champagne.'

'The real stuff or the crap?'

'The stuff we drank had Moët on the label, and it tasted real enough to me.'

'Moët, eh. It's about a ton and a quarter a bottle at Sonny's.'

'How much?'

'A ton and a quarter, or thereabouts.'

'Straight up?'

'Straight up.'

'Then the bill must have been well over a grand. They said they'd had a good week.'

'I bet they fucking did,' spat Brady.

'And that's not counting the coke we had. Seeley had a bagful big enough to choke a donkey.'

'You had some, did you?'

'What do you think? I had to. Protective colouring they call it. And next time I'm supposed to be paying. You'd better get me some scratch. I need all *my* money for my old age.'

'What, next year?'

'Very good. I'll have to remember that. So?'

'I'll get you some cash. Don't worry.'

'Good. Make sure you do.'

'Do you know when they're getting in touch?'

I shrugged. 'No. Seeley was too out of it when he dropped me off last night. But I'm working tonight. It's Saturday. They might pop in.'

'Right, I'll get you some cash tomorrow. Are you working?'

'Day off – all day.'

'Doing anything?'

'The *Observer* crossword. And catching up on lost sleep.'

'You *are* getting old. I'll be round about six.'

'You'd better give me your number, just in case.'

'Right,' he said, and went through his pockets until he came up with a scrap of paper. 'Got a pen?' he asked.

'Is this the new face of the Met then?' I said. 'High-tech, computer-literate, but still short of a biro?'

'I'm old-fashioned.'

I shook my head and found one, and he scribbled down three numbers. 'Home, car and bleeper,' he said. 'Twenty-four hours a day. Like you said, high-tech.'

'I am impressed,' I assured him.

'I'd better split,' he said. 'Things to do.' He finished his coffee and left. I made more tea and read the paper until it was time to get ready for work.

17

I was on time for work that night. Early in fact. I rolled in about six. The place was fairly full, and JJ and the two barmaids were busy.

'Want a hand?' I asked.

'Clear the tables will you, Nick?' said JJ. 'It's been a bloody nightmare in here this afternoon.'

I took off my jacket and got stuck in. At six-thirty the shifts changed. That Saturday night we had a chef on, JJ worked the restaurant, and I ran the bar with one barmaid. By eight the place was buzzing. At eight-thirty Seeley and Hughes arrived. They came straight over to me.

'Can we have a table?' asked Hughes.

I looked through. One couple was just leaving and there was no one else waiting. 'Sure,' I said. 'No problem. Want a drink?'

'Two Pina Coladas,' said Seeley. I knew it. I knew eventually they'd have to have Pina Coladas.

'I'll bring them through.'

'Take a break. Join us,' said Hughes.

'It's a bit busy right now.'

'Join us,' said Hughes, and his tone was almost menacing. 'We need to talk.'

I didn't like the sound of that one bit. 'I'll see what I can do,' I said. 'Go through and sit down. I won't be a minute.'

I checked with the barmaid as I made their drinks. 'Can you manage on your own for a minute?' I asked.

'I'll cope,' she said.

I took the drinks through to their table.

'Sit down, Nick,' invited Hughes.

'I haven't got much time.'

'You've got time for this. I've been hearing some funny things about you.'

That sounded ominous. 'Such as?' I said, pulling out a chair.

'Such as you used to be a copper.'

'Is that all? I suppose Kylie told you.'

'Yes. She told me last night after you'd gone. She thought I'd know.'

I shrugged. 'It's no secret. Did she also tell you I was busted out of the force?'

'Yes.'

'And it's true. Years ago. That's all finished with now. What's the problem?'

'Once a copper . . .' said Hughes.

'You reckon. I've got news for you.'

'What did you get busted for, Nick?' asked Hughes. As if he didn't know.

'Didn't Kylie tell you that, too?'

'*You* tell us,' he said.

'For stealing from the evidence lock-up.'

'What kind of evidence?'

'Evidence from a drugs bust. Cocaine.'

'How much?'

'Enough.'

'And?'

'And what?'

Hughes looked at Seeley. 'What did you do with it?'

'I used some. I sold the rest.'

'And you got captured?'

I nodded.

'Didn't they prosecute?'

I had to laugh, though it wasn't funny. 'No,' I said.

'They didn't need the publicity. It was all hushed up. They let me resign, and I lost my pension.'

'Who did you sell the drugs to?' asked Seeley.

'A contact.'

'Who?'

'Do leave off.'

'Nick, listen. Be reasonable. You saw what we had last night?'

'So?'

'It was part of our stock.'

I looked around the restaurant. 'Do you think this is the right place to talk about stuff like that?'

'Where better?' asked Seeley. 'It's noisy. No one's listening.'

'I still don't know what it's got to do with me. Your business is your business. I just want a quiet life.'

'Nick,' said Seeley. 'We know you didn't get that motor you're driving by serving beer in this dump. You've obviously got a pedigree.' From him I suppose that was a compliment. 'We buy and sell. Now, if you know a buyer . . .' He left the sentence unfinished.

'Yeah.'

'You could do yourself a bit of good. Do us all a bit of good. So, what's his name?'

I pretended to think about it for a minute. 'Brady,' I said.

'Where's he based?' asked Hughes.

'Kennington.'

'Shifts a lot, does he?'

'He has his moments.'

'Could we make a meet?'

'I don't know.'

'But you could ask.'

'Sure.'

'And Nick.'

'Yeah.'

'It had better be kosher, or you're dead.'

'It's kosher. Don't worry,' I said. Fucking hell, I thought. I wish I'd never started all this.

By then I was getting dirty looks from JJ and the barmaid, so I made my excuses and went back to work. Seeley and Hughes had their meal, paid the bill and left.

As he went out, Hughes called me over. 'We'll be in touch,' he said. 'Get hold of your man. We can all do well out of this, Nick.'

'Don't worry, it's done,' I said.

And so am I, I thought. If this little caper goes wrong.

18

The rest of the evening passed by without excitement. We finally cleared the place of the last drunk about eleven-forty. The last drunk was an Arsenal fan, as it goes, so I suppose it's not surprising he was always on the piss. When we'd tidied up, I had a final coffee with JJ. I knew he was dying to make some comment, so I let him.

'You're mixing with a funny lot lately,' he said.

'No more than usual.'

'That's not the way it looks to me.'

'I don't get this, JJ,' I replied. 'What's it got to do with you?'

'It's to do with me when you leave the bar when we're busy.'

'Do me a favour, JJ,' I said. 'I was only gone for a minute.'

'It seemed longer.'

'I didn't realise I had to clock on and off.'

'Forget it,' he said. 'I'm sorry I spoke.'

'And talking of time off,' I said. 'I don't want to work on Wednesday night. Is that OK?'

'Why?'

'I've got a date.'

'A date. With a woman?'

'Yes.'

'Christ, what's come over you?'

'Leave it out, JJ,' I said. 'I'm not in the mood. Just remember I won't be here Wednesday night, all right?'

'It's fine by me, Nick. I wouldn't dream of coming between you and a woman. I was beginning to wonder about your sex life.'

'Don't. Just cover for me on Wednesday. Now I'm off. I'll see you Monday.'

'Night, Nick,' he said, and I left. I hadn't brought the car that evening. I didn't mind the walk home. It wasn't far. I was used to avoiding the vomit and greasy chip papers that littered the streets on a Saturday night.

When I got home, I wasn't tired. I put some music on the stereo and made coffee and chased down half a dozen large Grand Marniers, and found a bit of hash hidden away in the bathroom cabinet and rolled a fat joint. Now that's how to get a good night's sleep.

I surfaced about ten and went down for the papers. When I got back I made sausage, egg, bacon, mushroom, tinned tomatoes and a fried slice, and ate it reading about what a soap-opera star was getting up to between the sheets with his brother-in-law. I took my second mug of tea over to the comfortable chair and got stuck into the crossword.

About three o'clock, I heated up a pizza in the oven and washed it down with a couple of beers. Then I finished reading the papers and waited for Brady.

He was dead on time. 'All right?' I asked.

'No problems,' he replied. 'I've just come from a meet with the boss. He sent you this.' He hauled a thick brown envelope out of the pocket of his leather jacket and tossed it to me. I opened it and pulled out a wodge of fifties and counted them. One thousand pounds exactly.

'Do I have to sign anything?' I asked.

'Yeah. I always carry a Metropolitan Police receipt book with me when I'm working undercover.'

'Endesleigh's getting very trusting.'

'You weren't thinking of ripping us off, were you?' he said with that mad look back in his eyes.

'No. I wasn't.'

'There you go, then. So what's new?'

I told him.

'Brilliant,' he said. 'I'm beginning to think the boss was right about you. We've been trying to crack that pair for months.'

'You should have called me earlier,' I said as drily as I could.

'How do you get in touch?'

'I don't. They get in touch with me.'

'That's not so good.'

'That's the way they wanted it.'

'Fair enough. But try and get a contact number if you can.'

'It'll be a mobile.'

'Yeah, I know. But it could be useful.'

'I'll see what I can do. Want a drink?'

'What you got?'

'Everything. I work in a bar, remember. I get it wholesale.'

'Jack Daniel's?'

'Now you're talking.'

And that, I'm afraid, was the end of Sunday night.

We drank two bottles of the stuff between us, and I poured Brady into a mini-cab at about midnight.

Then I went and threw up in the bathroom.

19

Monday I nursed a hangover all day, and fed it with coffee and aspirin. The big trouble with too much Jack Daniel's is that the aftertaste lingers forever.

I turned into the bar just before six-thirty. Mondays were always quiet. There were just two or three customers in, when I arrived. JJ was sitting at a stool, gazing into an empty coffee cup.

'Evening.' I said.

'You look rough.'

'Thanks.'

'Been on the piss?'

'Something like that.'

'You've had a couple of calls.'

'Who?'

'Dunno. They didn't say.'

I had a pretty good idea. 'Male or female?' I asked.

'Male.'

'No message?'

He shook his head.

'Well, I'm here now if they want me.'

He nodded, then mooched off to play with his motor-bike, and I took over. It stayed quiet. A few faces I knew dropped in and out. One of them bought me a cold beer, which helped my head. At twenty past seven the phone rang. 'JJ's,' I said when I picked it up.

'Nick?'

'Yeah?'

'Roy. Roy Seeley.'

'Hello, Roy,' I said.

'I've been trying to get you all day. That geezer you work with wouldn't give us your home number.'

'Policy of the bar, Roy. So, what can I do for you?' As if I didn't know.

'Did you speak to your man yet?'

'Yes.'

'Is he interested?'

'Could be.'

'Good. When can we meet?'

'You tell me.'

'Tomorrow?'

'You're keen.'

'Always, when there's business involved.'

'What time?' I asked.

'When can you manage?'

I looked at the roster pinned to the wall next to the phone. I saw that I was due to work the next evening, and also that JJ had crossed my name off for Wednesday night. 'Daytime,' I said. ''Til six-thirty.'

'Daytime it is, then. He lives in Kennington, you said.'

'Right.'

'Let's make it local to him. No point in inconveniencing the man. That'll do you, won't it?'

'Suits me.'

'Good. There's a wine-bar down by the Cross. Hold on.' The phone went dead as he covered the mouthpiece. I waited. 'Everly's,' he said when he came back on. 'Know it?'

'No.'

'You'll find it. It's opposite the Roebuck pub.'

'Fine.'

'It's open all afternoon. How does three o'clock suit you?'

'Depends if it suits him. I'll give him a bell. See if he's

about. Give me your number.' He did. It was an 0831 prefix. Mobile. 'I'll get back to you before closing,' I said.

'Good. I'll look forward to your call.'

'See you, then,' I said.

'Bye.' And he was gone.

I served a waiting punter and phoned Brady. I tried his home first. Alfie answered. 'Is Brady there?' I said. He didn't answer, just put down the phone with a clatter.

A minute later: 'Yeah?' I recognised Brady's voice.

'Sharman,' I said.

'Nicholas. How goes it?'

'Seeley was just on the blower.'

'Was he? That was quick.'

'He wants a meet.'

'I bet he does. When?' he asked.

'Tomorrow afternoon. Three o'clock.'

'Where?'

'There's a wine-bar near you. Kennington Cross. Everly's.'

'I know it. Three, you say.'

'That's right.'

'Couldn't be better. Come round for me at two-thirty. We'll drive down in my wheels. Put on a show.'

'If you say so,' I said.

'I do. I'll let the boss know. Tomorrow two-thirty, then.'

'Right. *And* he gave me a number.'

'Very good,' said Brady. 'Let's have it.' I read it out to him. 'Great, Nick. I'll see you tomorrow.' And he hung up. So did I.

I phoned the number Seeley had given me, about an hour later. I didn't want anyone to think that Brady was too keen. 'I've had a word,' I said when I got through. 'Three o'clock tomorrow is OK.'

'Sweet, Nick. We could all earn nicely out of this.'

'Hope so.'

'Me too. I've got a good feeling about this one. See you

there.' He broke the connection before I could answer. I didn't. Have a good feeling, that is.

20

I didn't sleep much that night. I just lay in bed thinking of the possible consequences of assisting the police in their enquiries. None of the alternatives were particularly attractive. But it was too late by then to consider bailing out. Much too late. And *that* alternative was possibly the least attractive of them all. I got up about eight. The only good news was that my hangover had gone.

I didn't have the patience to read the paper, and I didn't fancy breakfast, so I just made cup after cup of sweet tea and paced the flat like a prisoner in a cell. And the irony of *that* didn't escape me either.

By midday I was starving, but couldn't face eating, and I'd smoked my last cigarette, so I decided to take a drive and buy some more. I put on a tan wool Valentino for the meet. I thought I might as well look the part, at least.

I drove up to the river. There's a little bar on a wharf on the South Bank, not too far from where Brady lived, with tables outside and where no one knew me. I parked up, bought a beer and twenty Silk Cut, and sat in the fresh air to catch a little of the spring sunshine and try to relax.

I got a table as far away from the rest as possible, and watched the office girls feed the seagulls scraps of their sandwich lunches, and wished for the thousandth time that my life had taken a different turn somewhere. But it was pointless. We are what we are, and that's that. No amount of wishing can change it.

I sat, hardly touching the beer, for an hour and a half. At two-fifteen I left the remains of the bottle and went back to the car. I got to the estate where Brady lived ten minutes early for my appointment. As I turned into the street, I saw a tall, dark-haired geezer come out of the front door of Brady's house and get into a dark green Jaguar XJS parked outside. I drove the Cosworth past, turned right towards the end of the cul-de-sac and stopped out of sight of the house. Something, I don't know what, told me not to let the driver of the XJS see me. I stayed where I was until two-thirty, and then did a U-turn and drove back and parked at the kerb outside Brady's front door. The Jaguar was gone.

When I rang the doorbell, Alfie answered.

'Is he in?' I asked.

'No, but I'm expecting him at any moment.'

Ripping one off with a handsome stranger, I thought, whilst the mouse is away, you naughty boy. A bit of revenge for what you think Brady's up to. What's good for the goose is good for the other goose. Interesting. And dangerous too. But I didn't say a word.

'You'd better come in and wait, I suppose,' said Alfie, but I could tell he wasn't creaming his jeans at the thought.

Just then I heard the sound of a high-powered engine, and I looked round. Brady's Porsche swung round the corner and drew up in front of the Ford. The top was down, and his long hair was loose and tangled from the slipstream. He hopped out and bounded across the pavement. 'Right on time,' he said. 'Good. In you go.'

I went inside and he followed me, and we all stood awkwardly in the tiny hall.

'Upstairs, Alfie,' said Brady. 'Find something to do. I've got business to discuss with Nick. Then we're going out.'

Alfie tossed his head and did as he was told, but I could tell he wasn't happy.

92

'Through here,' said Brady, and led me into the kitchen. 'Coffee?' he offered.

'Sure.' There was an electric percolator plugged into the wall socket. He fetched down a mug from the cupboard and filled it. 'Milk?'

'Yeah – and one sugar.' I took the mug and perched on a kitchen stool and accepted one of his cigarettes and took a light.

'Right,' he said. 'This is the way it goes. You introduce me as the buyer. I'm the street man. The funky geezer. You know the type: a right arsehole. Of course, I have a principal. The money man. So I want a test sample now. Today. And when I report back that it's OK, I make a small purchase. And then, if that's good stuff, the biggy. That's when we move in and bust the fuckers. But it has to be a very big buy. Big enough to lead us to the top cockroaches. These two we're meeting today are trash. Scum. The only reason they're useful to us is that they can identify the ones we really want. And faced with a long time away, they'll do a deal. I know it. Shit, they'd peddle their grandmother's pussies to stay on the outside.'

'What about me?' I asked.

'You'll be looked after, don't worry.'

'But I do.'

'Trust me.'

'You're a doctor, I know.'

'What?'

'Nothing.' I looked at my watch. 'Are we fit then?'

'Sure.'

'Are you going to be carrying?'

'What?'

'What do you think? That cannon of yours, of course.'

He pulled his leather jacket open so I could see the holster he was wearing. 'I told you I always do.'

I looked up at the ceiling 'For fuck's sake,' I said.

'Don't worry. I keep telling you.'

93

'Trust me, I know.'

'That's right.' And the mad grin was back. I could never quite get to believe that grin. 'I'll just say goodbye to Alf,' he said. 'Gotta keep him sweet. You know how it is.'

I knew exactly how it was, but once again I said nothing. He got up and left the kitchen. He was only gone for a minute. When he came back he said, 'Come on then, if you're coming.' And we went out to his car.

'Will my motor be all right here?' I asked.

He laughed. 'You're worried about a *parking ticket*, with what you're into?' And he shook his head in disbelief.

I didn't bother to answer. I climbed into the passenger seat of his car. He started the engine with a roar, slapped the gear-stick into first, pulled round in a tight three-point turn, and away with a yip from the back tyres. We screeched into the Kennington Road and accelerated down towards the Cross and turned into Kennington Lane, and he pulled up at a parking meter opposite a parade of shops.

'Hardly worth bringing the car,' I said, when we'd stopped.

'I like to. It gives me a sense of security. That's us over there.' And he pointed.

The wine-bar was on the parade between an old-fashioned tailor's shop and a greengrocer. It was small, with a plate-glass window containing a menu chalked on a blackboard, and over the front '*Everly's*' was sign-painted in gold on a green background. Brady put the top of the Porsche up, and we got out of the car. He fed a few coins into the meter, and we crossed the road. I pushed open the door of the wine-bar at five to three.

It was a long, narrow room with a polished wooden bar running down the right-hand side. One punter was sitting on a stool in front of it, gazing into space. A big mirror ran down the wall opposite. The bar ended in a half wall. Beyond that, Everly's opened into a back room full of white tables and chairs. A *Commodores* tape was playing on the sound system.

Seeley and Hughes and a woman were sitting at a table in the far corner, as far away from the bar as was possible. The woman was sitting with them, but not close, whilst they talked. Her chair was pulled back from the table, and she was checking her make-up in the mirror of her compact. She was wearing a bright green two-piece suit. Seeing her there reminded me of Lana Turner in *The Postman Always Rings Twice*. The original version that turns up on TV every now and then, not the dopy remake. She had blonde, almost white hair, and she was hard-faced with it. Even from across the room I could tell that.

'They're here,' I said. 'Who's she?'

'His old woman,' replied Brady. 'Come on, introduce me. Don't forget, I'm not supposed to know them.' I led him through to the back. The two men looked up as we entered. The woman ignored us.

'Roy, Pat,' I said. 'This is Brady.'

Roy got up. 'Just Brady?' he said.

'That's right,' said Brady, and the grin appeared. Don't push it, I thought.

Roy shook his hand—and so did Pat, but he remained sitting down.

'Brady, Nick, this is my missus, Jools,' said Seeley.

'No, I'm not,' she said, still looking in the mirror and ignoring us.

'As good as,' said Roy.

'Yeah,' she said. Like it wasn't. But it was immaterial, anyway.

'Hello, Jools,' I said.

She looked at me for the first time, and she had that look in her eye that said: *Don't bother, son. You've got no chance.* But that look made you want to try all the harder. And she knew it. 'Hello, Nick,' she said. 'That's a nice suit. Are you wearing it for a bet?'

'Shut up, Jools,' said Roy.

'Sorry, I'm sure,' she said.

I had to laugh. 'Yeah, that's right,' I said to her.

'Well, you won,' she said, and winked at me.

I wondered what I'd won – and when I'd collect.

21

'So what are you drinking?' asked Seeley, rubbing his hands together like the original hail-fellow-well-met.

'What you got there?' said Brady. Pointing at the single bottle on the table.

'A rather fine Cabernet Sauvignon,' said Seeley.

'That'll do.'

'I'll get it,' said Seeley, and he went to the bar. Brady and I pulled up chairs and sat down.

'Nick here's been telling me all about you guys,' said Brady.

Hughes looked at me. 'Like what?' he said.

'Just what you told me,' I said.

'Fine,' said Hughes, shifting his shoulders under the slubbed silk jacket he was wearing.

Seeley came back with two bottles of wine and two more glasses. He made like mother, and I took a sip. It wasn't bad. I took out my cigarettes and offered them round. Only Jools took one. I lit both and she looked at me through the smoke they made. Green eyes, she had. Almost exactly the colour of her suit.

'So,' said Seeley to Brady. 'I understand you and Nick have known each other a long time.'

'Years,' said Brady.

'And you do a little business together.'

'A little,' said Brady. 'You've got to keep the wolf from the door, you know.' And he turned and fixed me with a stare.

'So true. And perhaps we can help you keep it even further away,' said Seeley.

'I don't know you,' said Brady. 'And I don't know her.' He moved his eyes over to Jools, which didn't seem to bother her in the least.

'She's all right,' said Seeley. 'She's with me.'

'And that's supposed to make me feel better?'

'Do you want me to go?' asked Jools.

'No,' said Seeley. 'You stay where you are.'

She shrugged.

'Let's get one thing straight,' said Brady. 'I'm only here because Nick told me you were OK. I didn't come to be sociable. I'm interested in one thing and one thing only. Profit.'

'I think Nick can testify to the quality of our product.' Seeley again.

'He has. But that was your personal stuff.'

'What we sell is of the same calibre.'

'I doubt that,' said Brady.

'There's only one way to find out,' interjected Hughes.

Brady sniggered. It wasn't a pretty sound. 'Listen,' he said. 'We all know there are degrees of quality. I don't doubt that any sample you show me will be excellent. But quantity merchandise is sometimes a different story, and I don't want to be left holding a bunch of duff gear, now do I?'

There was silence at the table, and *The Commodores* tape had finished and been replaced by Roy Orbison.

'I guarantee that won't be a problem,' said Seeley.

'That's what they all say,' said Brady, and the expression on his face told us all what Seeley could do with his guarantee.

'So what do you suggest?' asked Hughes.

'You *have* got a taste with you?'

'Sure,' said Hughes.

'OK. I live just around the corner. I have everything

98

there I need to test the stuff. If it comes up to my bench-mark, we're in business for a buy. But just a small one.'

'And?' Hughes again.

'If that's of the same quality, I can shift all you can supply.'

'I doubt that,' said Hughes.

'Try me.'

'Perhaps we will.'

'Let's go, then,' said Brady. 'Get out the old chemistry set.'

'Fine,' I said, and started to get up.

'We don't all need to go,' said Hughes. 'You stay here with Jools.' I looked at her, and she looked about as happy as if she'd just found a scorpion in her panty drawer.

'If that's OK,' I said.

'I couldn't care less,' said Jools. That was obvious.

'Later,' said Brady, and the three of them left.

When the door had shut behind them, she said, 'Did you enjoy your evening at Sonny's?'

I looked at her.

'Don't worry. I know all about what Roy gets up to when I'm not around.'

'It was OK,' I said.

'I wouldn't bother taking your friend with you next time.'

'Why's that?'

'He's bent, isn't he?'

I nodded. 'Very observant of you.'

'Thought so.'

'You can tell?'

'Usually. *You* aren't.'

'No,' I agreed.

'You don't swing both ways?'

I shook my head. 'No,' I said.

'I'm pleased to hear it. He doesn't like women much, does he?'

99

I almost said that I didn't know him that well, but bit down on my tongue just in time. I'd have to watch things like that. 'Depends on the woman,' I said instead.

'Cheers. Can I have another cigarette?'

'Sure.' I offered her the packet, and she took one, and so did I. I left the packet open and put it on the table. 'Help yourself,' I said.

'Thanks. Roy tells me you met him in a bar.'

'He met me. I work there. I've got the same car as he has.'

'That bloody thing. He can't handle it. He'll kill himself some day.'

I made no comment. 'I've never seen you there with him.'

'Roy doesn't take me out much.'

'Why not?'

She shrugged. 'Who knows?'

'Well, he's brought you today.'

'Lucky old me.'

I filled her glass.

'Are you trying to get me drunk?'

'No.'

'Pity.'

In the background Roy Orbison sang 'Only the Lonely.' Dum Dum Dum Dumee Doo Wah.

I smiled. 'Are you two getting married?'

'Whatever gave you that idea?'

'Roy said . . .'

'Roy says a lot.'

'So you're not?'

'Who knows?'

And that just about said it all. We stayed there drinking and smoking for another fifteen minutes or so, until the rover boys returned. Seeley and Brady were chatting away like old friends. Hughes looked as morose as ever. Brady stopped at the bar and ordered champagne.

'I take it everything went OK,' I said, when he came over with the bottle and a handful of fresh glasses.

'Better than.'

'Good. Deal done?'

'Looks like it.'

'Fine. Then you won't need me again.'

'Don't you believe it. You haven't even started yet. You're going to be the messenger boy. Just to keep everything in the family.'

'That will be nice.'

'Come on guys,' said Seeley. 'No secrets. We're all friends now.'

'Just putting Nick in the picture,' said Brady.

'Fine,' said Seeley and raised his glass. 'Here's to Brady and Nick. I think we're going to do great things together.' Seeley was rapidly getting to be a big pain in the arse.

Brady raised his glass in return. 'And here's to Roy, Pat and Jools. I hope you're right.'

I saw Jools's mouth twist sardonically, but she raised her glass with the rest of us.

When the bottle was empty, I said I had to leave. Brady checked his watch and said he'd come along with me. We said our farewells and left. I felt Jools's eyes burning into my back as we went through the door.

22

Brady gave me a lift back to my car, 'I'm going to need to talk to you soon,' he said.

'I'm working tonight.'

'Tomorrow?'

'Day off – but I'm busy in the evening.'

'I'll call you in the morning, buy you lunch.'

'I can hardly wait.'

'Don't worry. It'll all be over soon.'

'Tell me about it.'

'I will, tomorrow.'

I left him and went back to my car, and drove home, and got ready for work.

It was an uneventful evening. Nice and quiet and I didn't see anyone I knew except maybe to say hello to. That suited me fine.

As I had all Wednesday off, I took a spare set of keys home so that I could open up on Thursday morning.

The next morning the phone rang about eleven. It was Brady. 'You fit?' he asked.

'For just about anything.'

'Good. Listen, I've got an errand or two to run. I'll pick you up in an hour.'

'I'll be here.'

'Fine,' he said, and hung up in my ear.

The doorbell rang at twelve o'clock precisely. I grabbed a jacket and went downstairs. When I opened the front door Brady was leaning against the porch wall, smoking a cigarette.

'Morning,' he said.

'Morning,' I replied, and closed the front door behind me.

'We'll take my car,' he said.

'Fine by me.'

We walked to his Porsche, standing at the kerb, and climbed in. When he turned on the ignition, something jazzy and Hammond-organ-led oozed out of the speakers. I fastened my seatbelt.

'What's the story?' I asked.

'We've got to talk about our mutual friends and what's happening.'

'I was afraid of that.'

'You worry too much, Nick. You'll get ulcers.'

'I should live that long.'

'You will. So, what about lunch?'

'OK. If it's your treat.'

'It is. Where do you fancy?'

'I'm easy.'

'So I heard. I'm fucked off with South London. Hampstead suit you?'

'Fine,' I said. 'I've had some very expensive lunches in Hampstead.'

He grinned and selected a gear, revved up the engine, and the car burned rubber when he dropped in the clutch.

The way he drove, it didn't take us long to get to the river, then we got caught in a long jam through Holborn, but that more or less cleared by the time we got to Camden Town and we drove up Haverstock Hill to reach Hampstead High Street just after twelve-thirty.

Brady chose the Dôme for the first stop. He parked his car in a back street behind the main road, and we walked to the bar.

Inside it was crowded with rich kids and their boy/girl

friends, and au pairs looking for a rich kid of their own, and middle-aged women who had once been rich kids themselves and were trying to remember what it was like.

There were no seats free until two of the au pairs, tired of the game, finished their orange juices, paid, and slipped off their stools at the bar. Brady and I moved in and took them, just beating off a pair of eighteen-year-old boys in five-hundred-quid leather jackets.

We ordered a beer each and I looked around. From where we were sitting I could see through the foldback windows at the front which had been opened wide to make the bar part of the street outside, and which let in the Hampstead dirt, road noise and petrol fumes on a slight breeze from the south.

'I had a long talk with the boss last night. He's very pleased the way things are going,' said Brady.

'I'm glad someone is.'

'Meaning you're not?'

'Not particularly. Why do I have to mule the merchandise?'

'Simple. I'm not supposed to know those two arseholes. They don't know me. We all know you. You're the ideal man for the job.'

'I only met the pair of them last week. What do they know?'

'A lot about you, from what I could gather yesterday. They've been doing a bit of checking into your background.'

'Is that right?'

'Certainly is. And they're well impressed. They think you're the business.'

'So I'm the mug that gets nicked.'

'Amongst others.'

'Couldn't I just slip away in the confusion.'

'We'll see.'

I bet we will, I thought.

About then Brady seemed to get bored with the

conversation and swung round on his seat to regard the rest of the clientele of the bar. 'This place sucks,' he said.

'You chose it.'

'Yeah, I know. You want to eat here?'

'No thanks. If you're going to buy me lunch, I want to go somewhere that's that got four walls and a better wine list.'

'I didn't expect snobbery from you. Not when you work where you do.'

'You'd be amazed,' I replied.

'OK,' he said. 'Let's have another beer and then find a restaurant.'

'Suits me,' I said.

We got more beers and poured them. Outside a car pulled up at the kerb. It was a gunmetal-grey Six series BMW. From where I was sitting I could read the number-plate: SPL1F. So could Brady. Two black guys got out. The driver was huge, with locks and a shell suit. Green, orange and black. The passenger was smaller. Slimmer. Sharp in a double-breasted suit, shirt and tie. Shiny shoes and short neat hair.

Brady clocked them and his face darkened. 'I hate that shit,' he said. 'Splif, I ask you. Fucking schwartzes. They've always got to spoil it by being flash.'

A young punter in the bar – handsome, blond, wearing expensive sweats – saw the two blacks and left his coffee and went outside. Brady and I watched him go up to them.

'They're doing a fucking deal,' said Brady. 'Fucking bastards. In broad daylight. Jesus I don't believe this.'

'Believe it,' I said.

That seemed to make him even madder, if anything. 'Fuck that shit,' he said. 'I'm not going to let them get away with that. Taking the piss.'

'Brady,' I said. 'You're supposed to be a drugs dealer yourself. A drugs dealer out to lunch. If you want to do anything, call the police.'

'Fuck that,' he said again. 'No one knows me round here. I'll do it myself.' He stepped off his stool. 'Watch and learn, son,' he said, and pushed through the crowd to the door of the bar. I stepped off my stool, too, and went to the open window. A young girl in a window seat with a glass of Coke and that day's *Mail* open in front of her looked up at me. I smiled down at her. She didn't smile back. I shrugged. What the hell, I thought. No one's charm works all the time.

Brady went up to the trio. 'Police,' he said. The young white guy looked sick and stepped back a pace. 'Stand still,' said Brady. 'You as much as move a muscle and you are in some deep shit, believe me.'

The boy said nothing. 'Do you hear me,' Brady screamed into his face. All of a sudden the people in the bar started taking notice.

The boy nodded. His face was pale.

Brady turned to the two black guys. 'You,' he said to the smaller one. 'Empty your pockets.'

'What,' the black geezer replied. 'Are you sure?'

Brady slapped him round the face hard. 'Don't fuck with me, cunt,' he shouted. His face red and mad-looking. 'I'm a police officer. Empty your pockets.'

'I don't have to . . .' said the black guy, and Brady grabbed him and shoved him against the car. Then the driver decided to make a move and grabbed Brady's arm. Brady turned and chopped him on the side of the neck with the other hand, almost casually. Then he took hold of a handful of his locks and started slamming his head against the top of the car. I suddenly realised how strong he was. The driver was massive but he didn't have a chance. Brady just kept picking up his head and whacking it down on top of the car until the roof of the BMW was dented with the force of the blows, and blood started leaking from the big guy's nose and ears and splashing over his shell suit and Brady's jacket. After fifteen or twenty seconds of that treatment, Brady stopped and let him go, so he staggered around glassy-eyed and dazed.

It was then I realised that Brady was quite mad.

'Now empty your fucking pockets,' Brady screamed at the smaller guy, who this time did as he was told. A wallet, handkerchief, small change appeared, and Brady took them and threw them on to the bonnet of the car. Then it started to get interesting. First the guy took out a knife. A switch-blade with a mother-of-pearl handle. Brady dropped it into the gutter and stamped on it with his Doc Marten's boot until it broke into four or five pieces. The black guy looked sick. Brady snapped his fingers, and reluctantly the black guy took half a dozen white paper wraps from his shirt pocket. Brady bared his teeth and let them slip between his fingers on to the pavement, and ground them into the concrete with the heel of his boot until the paper disintegrated, and still he kept grinding the white powder until it was mud.

'Now get into the car, both of you, and get lost, and never let me see your faces round here again.'

They did as they were told. The smaller bloke took the wheel. I doubt if his minder could see, let alone see to drive. As the car pulled slowly away, Brady lashed out with his foot at the rear number-plate. He must have had steel toe-caps on his DMs, as it cracked from the force of the kick but it didn't seem to hurt his foot at all.

Then he grabbed a handful of the blond guy's sweat jacket. 'Go!' roared Brady. 'Go now. And don't let me see *you* here again either.'

The blond boy didn't need to be told twice. He turned around and nearly ran down the hill in the direction of Camden Town.

Brady came back into the bar. It was silent. We had no difficulty in getting our seats back at the bar. The other customers were only too pleased to give us plenty of elbow-room. A lot of the punters headed towards the front door and some of the others in the direction of the washrooms.

'Lots of toilet action now,' said Brady with a grin, as he picked up his glass. 'Mostly women. Flushing all sorts of stuff that their chickenshit boyfriends have given them. You'll be able to get stoned drinking the water in the Ladies in a minute.'

'I think I'll stick with the beer,' I said.

23

By that time the staff in the place were giving us *very* weird looks and starting to whisper to each other.

'I think we'd better go,' I said.

'You reckon?'

'Unless you want to get involved with the local Old Bill.'

'I'd rather eat lunch.'

'Let's go, then.'

'OK.'

We drank up and left. I felt every eye in the room on us as we went. 'Where to?' I asked when we got outside. To tell you the truth, I just fancied getting off the street quick. I really didn't care where we went. The whole business was beginning to get to me.

'Chinese?' asked Brady.

'That'll do.'

We walked up to the corner. On the next street, out of sight of the bar, was a Pekinese restaurant. It looked OK from the outside. We walked in and I sighed with relief. The main man came perambulating over and showed us to a table in the corner, behind an overgrown cheeseplant. It was quiet inside, so we got one meant for four. I can't stand eating at little tables. The waiter came over with the menus and we ordered up a pair of G&Ts and a couple of rounds of prawn crackers to be going on with.

I scanned the menu and knew exactly what I wanted. I'm a sucker for sweetcorn and crab-meat soup. I can't resist it. After that I fancied prawns in chilli sauce, soft noodles in a soup, and stir-fried vegetables. Brady wanted butterfly prawns and spring-rolls, then he wanted to ponce around with the crispy duck, so I said I'd have a bit – but I always eat too many of the pancakes and spoil the rest of the meal. Then he chose crispy fried beef, Szechuan-style sweet and sour pork and egg fried rice. No one was going to go hungry at our table, that was for sure. The waiter came over and we ordered. Plus Brady asked for a bottle of house white. The waiter left us to our gins and scurried off to the kitchen with our order.

'You were getting very friendly with Seeley yesterday,' I said.

'Prat. I'd like to wring his scrawny little neck. You were getting pretty friendly with *Jools*. His wife, indeed.'

'So what's all that about?'

'Christ knows. She's just some old slapper he pulled out of a whorehouse somewhere. That's his game.'

'Maybe it's love,' I said.

'Don't ask me,' he said. 'I never could understand heterosexuals. Anyway, whatever she is, don't be getting *too* pally. I hear he's a jealous man.'

'Don't worry,' I said. 'I won't. She's not my type.' Which was a lie. 'She asked me if I was gay like you.'

'She sussed me out, did she?'

'In a minute.'

He shrugged.

'What do you reckon to Hughes?' I asked, changing the subject.

'A real charmer. I wouldn't trust him with a stick of gum. He's the one to watch. He's carrying, too.'

'Is that right?'

'Yeah. Didn't you notice?'

'Out of practice,' I said. 'Do you think it was him that killed your two men?'

'We don't know. If we had evidence, don't you think

112

we'd move on him without all this play-acting?'

'Well, do you think it was one of his firm?'

'I keep telling you, we don't know. They're not the only targets that the squad are chasing. It could be any of them. Or none of them. Now, don't keep asking stupid questions.'

'OK,' I said. 'Keep your shirt on. Tell me what happened yesterday.'

'I tested the stuff they had with them. Good gear. Top of the range. But, like I said, you'd expect that. I ordered a kilo.'

'How much?'

'Thirty-five thousand quid.'

'Good deal.'

'A bargain. They think we could be doing a lot of business. Normally it would be cut by about a third and split into quarter-kilos and sold on at fifty a gram. But then you know all about that, don't you?'

'I know,' I said. 'Do you think it'll be the same quality as the sample?'

'You're talking like a real drug-dealer, Nick. You'll have to watch that. It really doesn't matter, does it. It's not going to be sold on. It'll be destroyed.'

'Sorry, I forgot. But playing along. How much are you going to buy in the really big deal.'

'10K'

'At?'

'Depends on how I hustle it. Between twenty-five and thirty a gram. Anything up to three hundred thousand.'

I whistled. 'That's a lot of money.'

'It's a lot of drugs,' he said. 'And a lot of porridge for the people who sell them. So I hope they do a lot of talking about who they're working for.'

'And I'll be in a lot of trouble,' I said.

He didn't reply.

'They'll want me dead, you know that,' I went on.

He shrugged and pulled a face. 'Not necessarily. Getting a pull is part of their job description. They're never going to know who blew the whistle. I'm not sticking around. I'll be gone to pastures new. They'll probably finger me as a grass. We just make sure you get bail and they don't.'

'They'll still be looking for me.'

'Too bad.'

'For *me*.'

'You'll survive, Nick. If you don't like the deal, we can always bring out the gun with your prints all over it.'

'I could always do a runner,' I said.

'You could always try.'

Just then the food arrived. We got stuck in. I took the pragmatic view of the whole thing. Hell, you've got to eat. And it was good, even if the company was a bit under the arm.

I pressed Brady for more details of the actual transaction, but he wouldn't play. 'We work on a need-to-know basis,' he said, touching the side of his nose. 'And right now you don't. You'll be told all in good time.'

We finished the meal and Brady paid from a wad of notes *that* thick, and he drove me back through town to my place. 'Got a date tonight?' he asked as he drew up in front of the house.

'That's right.'

'Your sex life is improving. See, things aren't *all* bad working for the Met.'

'I think I'd rather be celibate,' I said.

'Don't kid yourself.'

'I wouldn't dream of it.'

'Course you wouldn't. Listen, I'll be in touch soon. This thing'll be going down in the next few days. Keep yourself available. All right?'

'For you, always,' I said.

He grinned 'That's what I like to hear. Have fun tonight. Don't do anything I wouldn't.'

'Just the opposite,' I said, as I got out of the car.

24

That evening I drove up to town, parked in the NCP at Lexington Street, and walked round to the pub where I was due to meet Kylie. It was a chilly evening with a hint of rain in the air, so I took a light mackintosh with me to wear over my suit.

The Sun And Seven Cantons is a big old boozer on the corner of Beak and Great Pulteney Street. I arrived there maybe ten minutes early, got in a bottle of Bud, and took a seat at a table where I could watch both doors.

Kylie arrived at five past. Her thick blonde hair was swept back, her make-up was a masterpiece of understatement, and in the tan Burberry she was wearing with the Hermès scarf tied round her throat she looked about as much like a whore as my granny. She peered round, clocked me, smiled and came over. A couple of the male customers watched her as she crossed the carpet. I didn't blame them. I would have done the same myself in their shoes.

'Hello,' she said when she got close.

'You're looking good,' I said, and stood up. A proper gentleman. Mum would have been proud of me.

'Thanks.' She touched my hand briefly, then sat down.

I remained standing. 'Drink?' I asked.

'Sure.'

'Champagne?'

She smiled. 'I was a bit over the top the other night, wasn't I?'

'You might say that.'

'Was I bad?'

'The worst.'

'Did you mind?' she asked, and raised her eyebrows coquettishly. Some woman can play that game. Some can't. She could.

'Not at all. So, what are you drinking?'

'Vodka and tonic, please.'

I went to the bar and ordered her drink, and another beer for me. When I was back and seated opposite her, she said, 'I hope I wasn't late.'

'No.'

'Have you been here long?'

I tapped the first Budweiser bottle. 'That long,' I said.

'So you didn't mind waiting?'

'No.'

'So what are we going to do tonight?' she asked.

'Eat, drink and be merry, I suppose.'

'Sounds good to me.'

'Where shall we eat?' I asked.

'I don't care.'

'What do you like?'

'Anything.'

'In particular?'

'I'm not fussy. You choose,' she said.

'Italian?' I asked.

'I could go a pasta. Good for my figure.'

'I don't think you've got a lot to worry about on that score.'

'Thank you,' she said, and her eyes softened.

'Don't mention it. So, come on, then, it's your manor. Have you got a favourite Italian restaurant round here?'

'There's a good one in Wardour Street.'

'That's it, then.'

We finished our drinks and left the pub and walked through Soho. The streets were crowded and Kylie took my arm, but kept stopping and dragging me back to look in shop windows. I didn't mind in the least. Eventually we got into Wardour Street and found the restaurant. The maitre d' looked and sounded like Pavarotti, and welcomed Kylie like a long-lost relative. He tugged the rest of the staff out to show them who'd arrived, then slid us into a corner by the window at a table covered with a red-checkered tablecloth, and brought bread sticks, butter and a bottle of Chianti without being asked.

'You *have* been here before,' I said.

'Often.'

'What do you recommend?'

'The steak in red wine sauce is always good.'

'That'll do me. What about you?'

'Pasta in pesto sauce.'

I caught Pavarotti's eye and he loomed over the table and we ordered. He approved of our choice, and recommended the minestrone to start. We both concurred. The food was as good as she'd said and, after the first bottle of wine had vanished and a junior waiter had brought a second, we were chatting away like old friends. During the meal there was no mention of where we'd met or what we'd done. I finished up with an alcoholic zabaglione, and Kylie had Kiwi fruit flavoured ice-cream. By the time the coffee and brandies arrived, everything was copacetic. I looked at my watch: nine-thirty. 'Am I keeping you?' she asked.

'Course not. I was just thinking how time flies when you're having fun.'

'Liar.'

'It's true,' I insisted.

'Then I'm flattered.'

'So you should be. What do you want to do now?'

'I don't mind. What are the alternatives?'

'It's the wrong time for a film. Too early for a club. How about a drink?'

119

'Good idea, but the pubs'll be packed, and I hate that. How about my place? It's just round the corner and I've got a bottle of very good brandy and a coffee machine, and a pound of cap colombi.'

'Sounds perfect. As long as you think I'm house-trained enough to be trusted there.'

'Of course, I do. It's just that I don't usually mix business and pleasure.'

'And which am I?'

'Both. That's why I made an exception in your case.'

'Now I'm flattered.'

'And so you should be.'

I called for the bill and paid with plastic, and we left to effusive farewells from Pavarotti and his chorus, and many promises to return soonest. Her flat was only a few minutes' walk away, back past the garage where I'd left the car, by a men's shop in Brewer Street. The entrance was at the back, and we reached it through a dark and smelly little entry.

'This isn't too clever,' I said.

'I know. I'm always stepping over drunks sleeping it off.'

'Doesn't that worry you?'

'I can look after myself.'

'I hope so.'

'I'm here, aren't I?'

She used three keys to get through the solid-looking black-painted door at the back of the building. Once inside, with the door double-locked behind us, we were standing in a tiny, dimly-lit passage with a flight of narrow stairs at the far end. Our footsteps clattered on the uncarpeted wood as we climbed the first flight, then a second which brought us to another door. Two more keys opened it, and we went into a short hall with two doors off it: one to the left, one straight ahead. She pointed to the one on the side. 'That's the loo,' she said, then opened the other, which led into the sitting-room, with an open-plan kitchen on the left. Opposite was another door that I assumed led into the bedroom. This was confirmed when she took off her coat, then collected mine from me, and took them both through. I saw a dressing table in front of a curtained window, and the foot of a double bed. She dropped the coats on it and came back.

'Sit down,' she invited.

I chose the flower-patterned sofa that looked like it pulled out into a bed. She went into the kitchen and plugged in the coffee machine and filled the jug with water, and a filter paper with dark roast ground coffee. When it started to gurgle nicely, she took two small balloon glasses and an unopened bottle of brandy out of a cupboard above her head. She opened the bottle. 'Ice?' she asked.

'As it is,' I said.

'Me too.' She poured two generous measures into the glasses and brought them through. She kicked off her shoes and sat on the armchair opposite me. 'Got a cigarette?' she asked.

I took out my Silk Cut and she took one and I lit it for her. 'Nice place,' I said.

'It suits me.'

'Rented?'

'Yes. I like to move around.'

'Where were you before?'

She didn't reply to this, just stabbed out her cigarette in the ashtray on the table next to her chair, then said, 'The coffee'll be ready.' She got up and went back to the kitchen, where she poured two cups and brought them through on a tray with sugar and cream. 'Just like home,' she said.

'Better,' I said. 'I don't get treatment like this at home.'

'Aren't you married?'

I nearly choked on my coffee. 'Do I look married?'

'I don't know what married looks like.'

'Not like me, that's for sure.'

'You might be lying.'

'I might be, but I'm not. I *was* married, but not anymore. She's in Scotland now with hubby number two.'

'Was that your idea? A divorce, I mean.'

'No. My fault, but not my idea.'

'You don't sound too happy about it.'

'It's got nothing to do with happiness or anything else. It's unfinished business. Something that's never been sorted. After a bit people stop listening when you say you're sorry. They get apology fatigue, I suppose. So even when it's true they don't care.'

She nodded. 'Any children?'

'One. Judith. She's with her mother.'

'How old?'

'Twelve.'

'Do you see her?'

I shook my head. 'I haven't seen her since last year. It's my fault. But I think it's probably better that I don't. For her, I mean.'

'Do you miss her a lot?'

'Yes.'

'That's a shame.'

I nodded.

'Don't you have a girlfriend?'

I shook my head.

'A loner, eh?'

'I suppose so. Not exactly by choice. More circumstance. How about you?'

She looked round. 'There's no one here.'

'Is there anyone anywhere?' I asked.

'No.'

'Another loner.'

'That's right.'

'Two loners in Soho.'

'Sounds like a song,' she said.

'A pretty sad one.'

'Talking of songs, shall I put on some music?'

'What have you got?'

'Not much. I don't have much of anything. It weighs me down.' She got up and went over to the stereo system and started going through the pile of tapes. '*Genesis*?' she asked.

'I could live without them.'

'*Dire Straits*?'

'No.'

'Elton John, *Police*, Madonna, *The Beatles*.'

'Give me a break. Let's take a look.'

I put down my cup and went and joined her. I could smell her perfume again, and she rested her hip against mine. It felt solid and warm. I looked through the cassettes and found a Motown compilation and the latest Neville Brothers album. The stereo had twin tape decks, and I put in the two cassettes and pushed both play buttons. The first track was 'Tears Of A Clown' by *The Miracles* which I think I've only heard about a million times, but it still beat Phil Collins and Sting every way up. Kylie set the volume control and we went back and sat down again.

'Why did you ask me out?' she said.

'Who knows? We just seemed to hit it off.'

'Literally,' she said, and laughed.

'That's a strange place.'

'What, Sonny's?'

'That's right.'

'Very.'

'Have you worked there long?'

'No. Just a few months.'

I almost asked her if she liked it. What a dumb question. Next only to what's a nice girl like you doing in a place like that? I think she was half expecting me to. When I didn't say anything, she added, 'I've got to pay the rent.'

'Don't we all.'

'Is that why you work in a bar?'

'Partly. There's not that many jobs open to an ex-copper caught with his fingers in the till.'

'I can imagine.'

'I think you gave Pat Hughes a fright when you told him.'

'I know. I'm sorry about that. It just slipped out. I thought he knew.'

'I told you I'd just met them.'

'I *know*. I could have kicked myself. Too much champagne.'

'No harm done. It's no secret.'

'Have you seen him?'

'Both of them. Yesterday.'

'Business?'

'Yes.'

'I suppose I shouldn't ask what kind?'

'Definitely.'

'Don't get into trouble.'

'Would you care if I did?'

She nodded.

'Why?'

'I like you.'

'And I like you, too, Kylie.'

'Does that mean a fuck's not out of the question, then?'

She was right. It wasn't.

25

I woke up in the middle of a dream that I was a British POW digging my way to freedom, when the roof of the tunnel collapsed, trapping me under a ton of earth. I couldn't move my arms or legs and I could hardly breathe. When I opened my eyes, Kylie was sprawled on top of me, her face two inches from mine. I couldn't move my arms or legs and I could hardly breathe. I lay there for a second, trying to remember where I was, who she was, and who I was. Suddenly it all came back in a reassuring flood, and I managed to get some purchase on the sheet with one elbow and pushed her off me. As she moved away she opened one eye and looked at me.

'Morning,' I said.

'Hello there,' she replied. She looked a mess. Her thick blonde hair was tangled, and she hadn't removed her make-up when we'd come to bed, and the remains of it was smeared all over her face. 'I must look a mess.'

'No,' I said. 'You look great.' I lied about the former, but not the latter. She did look great. Tangled hair and smudged make-up, or no tangled hair and smudged make-up.

'I've got to pee. I'm bursting,' she said. Pushing back the bed clothes, she found a towelling robe on the dressing-table stool, pulled it on and left the room. As she went, I saw enough bed-warm, slightly damp, pneumatic flesh jiggling around to get me interested. More than interested in fact. I looked at the clock on the table by the bed.

125

Eight-five it read. I rolled out of bed myself, and pulled back the curtain at the window just enough to check what was going on outside, but not enough for anyone to see in. I didn't want to get done for indecent exposure, after all. And I certainly was. Indecent, that is.

Two storeys below me, Brewer Street was thronged with fresh-faced citizens heading for work. I scratched the stubble on my chin and went back to bed.

Kylie returned a minute or so later, shrugged out of the robe, and joined me. 'Coffee's on.' And slid her hand down to my groin. 'Interesting,' she said when she'd found what she was looking for. 'You should get up.'

'I've been up,' I replied. 'I didn't like it.'

She took my hand with her other hand, and put it between her legs. It was hot and sticky down there. 'I meant up me, silly.' And she climbed on top of me again, and manipulated me inside her, and started to rub herself up and down. By that time I was so horny that I only lasted a minute or so, but it was worth it.

When it was all over, she said, 'There's nothing like a quick one in the morning. And that was a *very* quick one indeed.'

'Are you casting aspersions on my staying power, or what?' I asked. 'Because if you are, too bad. I think the earth moved for me that time.'

'Me too, darling,' she said and kissed me. 'I'm not complaining. At least I know I turn you on.'

'You do,' I said. 'Now, did someone mention coffee or was I mistaken?'

'Oh Christ, it'll be ready.' She was off me, out of bed again, into her robe and out the bedroom in a second. I got up after her, pulled on my shorts and T-shirt, and went to the loo. The living-room smelled deliciously of fresh coffee. When I got back, she stuck a cup under my nose.

'Thanks,' I said.

'So what are you doing today?' she asked.

'Working. I'm due to open the bar at half-ten. I'd better get going soon.'

'Shame.'

'I know.'

'Will you drop me off?'

'Where?'

'The Embankment. I'm going to the gym. There's a session at nine-thirty.'

'Christ,' I said. 'Didn't you get enough exercise last night?'

'No . . . Well, yes. But I wasn't working on the right muscles.'

'All right,' I said. 'It's your funeral. But I warn you I'm going as soon as I'm dressed.'

'I love a masterful man. Don't worry. It'll only take me a second to get ready.'

'I've heard that one before.'

We finished our coffee and went back into the bedroom. Whilst I put on the rest of last night's clothes, she put on a pink leotard over black lycra leggings, a sweat-suit, towelling socks and trainers, pulled a sports bag out of the cupboard and put in a towel and a bottle of shampoo, and picked up her handbag.

'Ready,' she said.

'Let's go, then.'

'Just a minute,' she said, and rooted round for a pen and a piece of paper. She scribbled something on it and gave it to me. 'My number here,' she said.

'I'm honoured.'

'You should be. Use it.'

'I will. I promise.' I put the piece of paper carefully in my pocket. 'Come on, then,' I said. 'Otherwise you'll miss your torture session.'

She smiled and kissed me. It could have got steamy again, but we both had other things to do. Pity.

We went downstairs to the street, unlocking and relocking the doors as we went, walked the couple of hundred yards to the car-park and found the Cosworth.

'Nice car,' she said appreciatively, and started opening and closing the glove compartment, fiddling with the seat and playing with the electric windows. 'Will you take me out for a drive soon?'

'Sure,' I said as I drove down the ramps from level to level towards the exit. I paid the overnight fee, negotiated my way through Soho, round Piccadilly Circus and down to the Embankment. The gym faced the gardens next to the Houses of Parliament. I pulled up at the kerb opposite.

'Thanks for the ride, Nick,' she said.

'I think it's me who should be thanking you, if my memories of last night are correct.'

'You're such a disgusting man, I don't know why I like you so much. But I do. When am I going to see you?'

'I'll call you,' I said. 'Before the weekend. We'll get together.'

'Make sure you do. I'm looking forward to it already.' And she leaned over and kissed me, grabbed her bags and jumped out of the car. The last I saw of her she was dodging the traffic to get over the road.

26

I drove home, got changed and went to work. The phone in the bar rang around two. I answered it. 'Nick. Brady.'

'Hello, Brady,' I said. 'What can I do for you?'

'I need to see you.'

'When?'

'Tonight.'

'Why?'

'Because I say so.'

'Give me a clue.'

'Not on the phone.'

Paranoia strikes deep. I sighed. 'I'm through at six-thirty,' I said.

'We'll go out for a drink, right?'

'Why not?'

'I'll pick you up at your place at nine.'

'You're the boss.'

'You said it.'

'How could I forget.'

'That's what I like to hear. Nine o'clock then. Be ready. Dress smart.' And he hung up in my ear.

At the appointed hour, I was standing at my flat window with the curtains open and the light out, smoking a cigarette and watching the street, when Brady's car roared up and squealed to a halt outside. I went downstairs and met him on the doorstep. In the light from the hall I saw that he was dressed in a dark suit, shirt and tie. It was the first time I'd seen him without his leather jacket. I'd put on my old standby navy Armani, a pale blue Paul Smith baggy shirt, and a dark blue silk tie with a predominantly mustard-yellow Paisley pattern, and highly-polished, black Bass Weejuns.

'Am I smart enough for you?' I asked.

'Very nice.'

'I'm so glad you approve. So, where are we going that I need sartorial advice from you?'

'The Dealing Floor. Know it?'

Course I knew it. A couple of years before, it had been *the* club. The hottest ticket in town for every city whizz-kid determined to make a splash and his fortune and retire before the age of thirty. Without a membership card you were scum. With one, you were king. But that was then, and this is now.

'I thought it had closed down,' I said.

'No, it's still there. It's not what it used to be, but then what is? You ever been there?'

'No. Not my scene.'

'Well, you're going tonight.'

'Why?'

'I thought I'd show you where the money you'll be giving Hughes and Seeley will end up.'

'Come again?'

'I'll tell you later. Come on, let's go.'

We got into his car and headed towards the city. We crossed Tower Bridge and turned east, and followed the river to Venice Wharf and the Venice Tower, one of the tallest buildings in London. It was lit up like a birthday cake, burning enough energy to supply a small town. It loomed above the adjoining cityscape like a pink and white and yellow colossus, and was visible ten minutes before we got there.

The Dealing Floor was on the top floor of the tower, forty storeys above London. The other thirty-nine floors belonged to a merchant bank whose head office was registered in Liechtenstein, and which had subsidiaries in Luxembourg, the Cayman Islands and Delaware. Interest on deposits was a couple of percentage points over base rate. A fine investment. But you shouldn't blink too often or you might just find your life savings floating offshore somewhere with a school of silk-suited sharks taking tasty chunks out of the old pension fund.

A few years ago you couldn't have got a parking space closer than half a mile away for jammed-up Porsches, Ferraris, Mercedes and Golf GTI cabriolets; the queue at the special lift that went straight up to the club was ten deep, with paparazzi firing off flash-guns like automatic weapons; and you could have bottled the perfume the air-conditioning pulled out of the place, and sold it for forty pounds an ounce.

But as the icy fingers of the recession crept up the river, freezing it into white caps, it even left its dirty fingerprints up there, so close to the gods.

So now you could park outside, have the lift all to yourself, and get the best table in the place any time, any night of the week.

We stood in the foyer behind a twenty-foot-high sheet of plate glass that cut the volume level of the music and allowed some conversation, and looked into the disco room. That night it was empty except for two or three punters at the bar, the DJ, half a dozen waitresses wearing not much but their underwear, and a sad-looking geezer in a tuxedo. There wasn't one table taken in the restaurant section, which had once been booked solid a fortnight in advance, and where you could watch a wall full of big-screen TVs showing the share and currency prices on all the world markets any time of night or day. As the Tokyo market opened, breakfast was served, and you could check the Nikkei Dow index and work out how much loot you'd made overnight as you dug into a kipper or bacon and eggs.

I thought I'd rarely been in a more depressing place in years. 'Slow night,' I said.

'Every night's the same.'

'Why don't they close down?'

'You can't just close a place like this.'

'Why not?'

'The boys wouldn't appreciate it.'

'What boys?'

'*The* boys. The guys who opened this place as a laundry for dirty money.'

'So you were serious. You reckon the people who own this building and this place are your drug barons we'll be dealing with?'

'Sure I do.'

'And you come here.'

'I've told you a dozen times, I like to know the territory. I come here a lot. I like it.'

'So this is what a laundry looks like?'

'Sure.'

'I think maybe the washing-machines broke down.'

'You said it. But they insist that the good times are coming back. Listen, you go in the quiet bar.' He pointed towards a set of smoked-glass double doors. 'And I'll fetch the boss and introduce you.'

'Who does he think you are?'

'Someone with a high disposable income.'

I did as he said, and pushed through the doors. Inside it was *very* quiet, and deserted except for a barman behind a chrome-covered bar, polishing a glass as if he was trying to wear it out.

'Evening,' I said as I entered.

'Good evening, sir,' he replied. 'What can I get you?'

'How about some excitement.'

'We're fresh out,' he replied.

'OK. A Tom Collins will do, then.'

He reached behind him for the bottle of gin, and I sat

down at an ornate, leather-upholstered captain's chair, and watched as he mixed the drink. Before he was finished, Brady came into the bar with the geezer in the tux. 'Nick Sharman,' he said. 'This is Derek. He runs the place.'

'Welcome, Mr Sharman,' said Derek, and stuck out his mitten. I took it and we shook hands. 'It's always good to see friends of Mr Brady's. Almost like old times.' He looked round the empty room. 'Christ, but it's dead in here,' he remarked. Then, to the barman, 'Put some music on, Mikey. Liven the place up a bit. You could store bodies in here.'

'It *is* supposed to be the quiet bar,' said the barman petulantly.

'But not the morgue. Put on some music. There's a good boy.'

The barman shrugged and reached down and pushed some buttons, and Anita Baker's voice oozed softly out of the speakers.

'That's better,' said Derek. 'Get me my usual, and . . .' He turned to Brady 'What do you want, Mr Brady?'

'Scotch,' he replied.

'A large scotch, and whatever Mr Sharman's having. Stick them on my tab.'

'Thanks,' I said as the Tom Collins arrived. It was perfect. I felt it was up to me to say something. 'Nice place.' It was all I could think of.

'Used to be,' he said sadly. 'Dead now.'

'Things'll get better,' I ventured.

'Are you serious? I keep the doors to the roof double-locked now, so many punters threatened to jump off. The city's dead, my friend. And when the city's dead, the country isn't far behind.'

'Leave it out, Derek,' said Brady. 'We're supposed to be here to enjoy ourselves, not top ourselves. It's Nick's first time, so why don't you show him the dance floor?'

'What?' I said, wondering why the hell I'd be interested.

'Good idea,' said Derek. 'Come on, Mr Sharman. It'll give you a kick, I promise.'

I shrugged. 'OK,' I said to Derek. 'You coming?' to Brady.

'I've seen it. I'll stay here with this drink and the nice barman.'

'Sure,' I said.

I followed Derek out of the quiet bar, over the smooth carpet, and into the club proper that was still shaking to the music. I suppose another two or three people had arrived since we'd come in. But not enough to make the place look even slightly busy. The TV screens still pumped out their columns of figures, but no one even pretended to be interested.

We walked across the empty space between the bar and the DJ's booth, up a flight of four wide steps, and suddenly we were walking on thin air, or so it seemed. I was looking straight down forty storeys, and my stomach lurched. There seemed to be nothing between me and the street below. Derek grinned for the first time, and leant over and bellowed in my ear, 'Six-inch-thick plexiglass. Clear as crystal. Strong as cement.'

The street that ran along the embankment below looked to be about half an inch wide, with its lamps like a string of fireflies. They followed the river, which resembled a piece of black mirrored glass, and on the opposite bank I could see blocks of offices and flats, and a vista of yellow light, neon and black shadows that reached to the hills of south London.

Derek beckoned me out of the disco. When we were back in the relative quiet behind the viewing window, and we could speak without shouting, he said, 'Amazing, isn't it? People take it differently. One or two have actually been physically sick. Others just freeze and have to be carried off. Some lie down and stay there for hours, with other people stepping over them. We found one geezer flat on his back in the road outside with a pair of bins, looking up the girls' skirts. Apparently he'd been there every night for months, wanking himself silly during the slow songs.'

'Weird,' I said.

We walked back into the quiet bar. Brady was getting into the scotch. I sat down next to him and picked up my drink. 'That's incredible,' I said.

'I knew you'd like it. I remember the first time I saw it.'

'The good old days,' said Derek sadly. 'But there's not much happens anymore. We used to hire it out the place to all sorts. Arabs, Germans, Colombians – you name it. We've had orgies in here. A thousand people groping, sucking, fucking. You'd never believe it. Dogs. Pigs – you name it. We even brought a donkey up in the lift once. Shat all over the place. Donkey shit don't 'alf stink. I videotaped every one. Got them all in my office. For insurance, you know. You'd be amazed some of the people whose cocks and cunts I've got on film in there. One day I'm going to splice all the juiciest bits together and sell it. I'd make a fortune.'

'If you live that long,' said Brady.

'One of the reasons I haven't done it so far. We've got videos in the toilets, too. Now, that's even more interesting. Funny how many people pick their noses when they're taking a shit. And worse.'

I made a mental note to hold my water as long as possible.

'Let's have another round,' said Brady, and the barman got to it. When we were served, Brady said, 'You'll have to excuse us, Derek. Business, you know.'

'Of course, Mr Brady,' said Derek. 'I have to check the front of the house anyway, to make sure no one's dying of excitement. I'll see you gentlemen later.'

'Later,' said Brady, and Derek left us to our fresh drinks. 'Let's sit over there, Nick,' said Brady, and we moved to a table in the corner, furthest from the bar.

When we were comfortable, with cigarettes lit, he said, 'The first buy is tomorrow night.'

'Just as well I'm not working, then,' I replied.

'Just as well, or you'd have to be sick, wouldn't you?'

I didn't answer the question. We both knew the answer anyway. 'Where?' I asked instead.

'I'll let you know tomorrow when I bring the cash round.'

'Aren't you taking the secrecy aspect of this thing a little too far?' I said.

'Two guys died because they didn't. I don't want to be another . . . Or you, for that matter,' he said as an afterthought, which wasn't exactly reassuring. 'Don't worry, I'll take care of everything. I'll be at your place about ten with the dough. Be ready.'

'Am I ever anything else?'

'That's my boy.'

'You don't think Hughes or Seeley will pull any stunts, do you?' I asked.

'Not this early in the game. Later, who knows?' I didn't like the way he said it. But then I didn't like anything about the whole deal. He picked up my feelings. 'Don't worry, Nick,' he went on. 'Have a few drinks. Relax. Be like me.'

Anything I wanted less I couldn't imagine.

27

The next night was the first time that Brady was late. I
wondered if something had gone wrong, but I waited anyway.
What choice did I have? By the time he arrived I was sick
of waiting. Sick of everything that was happening. I was
in two minds whether to just forget the whole thing and go
out and get lost between the light and shadow of the London
night. Disappear into the gaps where the real people don't
go. I would have liked just to vanish like a puff of smoke.
But I knew I couldn't. There was no place left for me.
Endesleigh and his little crew had me exactly where they
wanted me.

So I stayed.

Brady turned up just after ten-thirty. He seemed nervous
and spaced out. So what was new?

I was watching out of the window again when he arrived,
and I met him at the front door before he rang the bell. He
was carrying a small, cheap-looking briefcase. We went
upstairs together.

'I take it that's the money,' I said when we were inside
my flat, with the door closed firmly behind us.

'You take it right.'

'You had some problems getting it?' I asked.

'What makes you say that?'

'You look a little mussed around the edges.'

'I'll survive.'

I hoped that I would, too. 'Show,' I said.

He put the case on the table, and opened it. It was full

of cash in bundles held by elastic bands. The notes on top were wrinkled and used-looking. 'Thirty-five grand?' I said with a question-mark attached.

He nodded.

'It looks like more.'

'Small denominations,' he said. 'The way they wanted it. You want to waste time counting it?'

I took his word for it. 'No,' I said. 'What time's the meet?' I asked.

'I don't know.'

'What does that mean? You must know.'

He didn't answer.

'Where is it?'

'I don't know that either.'

'So what the fuck do you know?'

'I know I've got to give you the money, and you go to Lambeth High Street. You know it?'

'I know it. Down by the river, right?'

'That's the one. There are two phone-boxes about halfway down. Wait by them, and you'll be contacted.'

'What happens if someone's using them?'

'Wait.'

'If there's a queue?'

'Jump it.'

'This is fucking Mickey Mouse, Brady, you know that?' I said angrily. 'Why can't they just come round here, do the deal, and go home?'

'That isn't the way they want it.'

'They're setting me up. I fucking know it,' I said. Or *you* are, I thought.

'For that?' he said, nodding scornfully at the briefcase on the table. 'That's nothing. Maybe next time, when the real money comes out. But not for thirty-five grand.' He made it sound like a pittance.

'I don't like this,' I said. 'I don't like this one little bit. Are you going to have me followed?'

He shrugged. 'We'll have to see how it goes.'

'Meaning no.'

'Meaning we'll have to see how it goes.'

'Jesus Christ! What you're saying is I'm totally dispensable.'

'You knew that already.'

Maybe I did, but it didn't make me feel any better saying it out loud. 'I'm not going to forget this,' I said.

'Whatever. Now, why don't you get going. You're supposed to be there at eleven-fifteen. It doesn't give you much time.'

I looked at my watch. It didn't. If there was a hold-up I wouldn't make it at all. So I went.

'I'll be here when you get back,' he said.

If I get back, I thought. 'Make yourself at home,' I said.

'I intend to.'

I took the briefcase, went downstairs, put the case in the boot, got into the car, and headed towards Vauxhall, then north along Albert Embankment, and turned right into the High Street. I pushed the car all the way, and it took me a lot less time than it should to get there. Halfway along the street, I spotted a pair of phone-boxes on the right-hand side, deserted, with their yellow lights beckoning like beacons. I drew up next to them, and got out of the car. I left the driver's door open and the engine running. By my watch it was eleven-twelve. There was no one about, and the street was as deserted as an abandoned film set, and felt about as real. The card phone had an official BT sticker on the outside declaring that it was out of order. I lit a cigarette and waited. The card-phone phone rang dead on time. The sound echoed down the street like a death knell. I answered. I knew exactly who the bell tolled for. Me.

'Hello,' I said.

'Sharman?' It wasn't a voice I recognised.

'Yeah.'

'Are you alone?'

'Yeah.'

'Got the package?'

'Yeah.' Again.

'There's another phone-box by the War Museum. In Lambeth Road, opposite the Churchill Clinic. Know it?'

'I'll find it.'

'Get there now. You've got less than two minutes.' And he hung up.

'Shit,' I said, dropped the receiver, and ran for the car. I slapped the stick into gear, peeled away from the kerb, shot down Lambeth High Street, did an illegal turn across Lambeth Road, cutting up a van as I went – and getting an angry blast from its horn for my troubles. I stayed in second and felt the G-force as the car hit sixty-five in the bus lane. I jumped the amber traffic light at the junction with Kennington Road, and pulled up opposite the telephone-box and jumped out of the car. I heard the phone start ringing as I ran across the street. A passing pedestrian stopped beside the box, undecided whether to answer or not, and I shouldered him out of the way with a 'Sorry'. I picked up the receiver. 'Sharman,' I said.

'That was very good.' It was the same voice again. 'Do you know Cleaver Street?'

'Sure.'

'That's your next stop.'

'Another box?' I asked. I was beginning to get tired.

'No. Go there, and turn right into Bowden Street. There's an old electronics factory on your left. You can't miss it. There's a For Sale sign outside. Go round the side. The fire door's open. Bring the cash. And be alone. We're watching you.' And he hung up again.

28

I drove round the block, and back down the Kennington Road to Cleaver Street. It was just by the Cross, at the back of the wine-bar where Brady and I had met Seeley and Hughes and Jools.

It was like going home.

I found the old factory with no trouble, parked the car, got the case and went in. The fire-door was just where the voice on the telephone had said it would be. And open, too. I walked inside. A very dim light lit the FIRE EXIT sign above my head. I stopped and listened. It was an old building with thick walls. Nothing.

In front of me was a flight of stone steps leading upwards. I took them. At the top was another fire-door. I pushed it open.

Inside was a big room. Empty except for the detritus of a factory that had shut down. A few wooden benches, tables, rubbish on the floor, yellowing page-three pin-ups on the walls. The usual. But with a big plus. Seeley and Hughes, and another face I didn't know, presumably the mystery voice on the phone, were standing in the faint light from three more FIRE EXIT signs, waiting for me. The stranger was another thick-set, hard-looking bastard in an expensive brown leather jacket, a roll-neck jumper, chinos and desert boots.

'Welcome,' said Seeley, like it was a marquee at Ascot.

'Hello, Roy,' I said. 'Pat. Who's your friend?'

The face said nothing. Nor did they. Another need-to-know scenario. And once again, obviously, I didn't. I let it go.

'Got the readies?' asked Hughes.

I held up the case.

'Let's have it.'

'Can I see the goods?' I asked.

There was another case on one of the benches. Better quality, by the looks of it, than the one Brady had given me. Free enterprise, see. Hughes opened it. Inside was a single, cloudy plastic package of white powder, about the same size as a bag of sugar. I picked it up and hefted it. Felt about right, weightwise. I put my case next to it. Hughes opened it. He picked up one of the packets of cash and riffled the notes.

'We'll have to count it,' he said almost apologetically.

'Be my guest. I'll need to check the merchandise.'

'Carry on,' he said.

All three set to work on the bundles. Brady had made it easy. There were thirty-five. It took them just minutes.

Meanwhile I stuck a fingernail through the plastic packaging round the coke, stuck in my finger and took a hit. It wasn't Domestos. In fact it wasn't half bad. 'Seems OK,' I said. 'I'm sure you'll hear if it's not.'

'It is,' said Seeley.

By this time they were satisfied the cash was all present and correct. We both closed each other's cases and picked them up. Done deal. Everybody ecstatic.

'You go first,' said Hughes. 'We'll see you later.'

'OK,' I said, and left.

The street outside was empty, but someone was playing opera on their stereo in one of the houses. Loud. Ain't culture wonderful?

I walked through a wash of sound to the car, opened it, threw the case in the back, and drove home. Nobody appeared to give a damn. I was there by twelve-thirty.

* * *

Brady was sitting in the dark on the sofa, drinking a beer and watching a black-and-white zombie movie on the TV. He looked just like one of the juvenile leads in the reflection from the screen. I switched on the light, and he squinted up at me.

'Got it?' he asked.

'Got it.'

'Let me see.'

I gave him the case. He opened it, found the split in the packet, and took a hit.

'Scientific,' I said.

He ignored me. 'This is good stuff,' he said. 'Just right.'

'Satisfied?'

'For now. I'll give it the proper test later.'

'Can you get it out of here, then?'

'Nervous?'

'A little.'

'You're safe. I'm the law, don't forget.'

Then God save us all, I thought. 'Even so . . .' I said.

'Can I finish my drink?'

'Of course.'

Before he left, I told Brady about the third party who'd appeared at the meet. He got me to describe him, down to the last detail I remembered. 'Don't know him,' he said. 'Maybe just a minder, but I'll check around. See if anybody else recognises him.'

'It was him that spoke to me on the phone.'

'Probably just testing that you'll take orders from strangers. But you never know. Don't worry. If anyone knows him I'll find out.'

He chugged down the last of his beer and got up. 'Don't bother to see me out, Nick. I'll find my own way.' He picked up the briefcase and headed for the door. 'I'll be in touch,' he said as he closed it behind him.

I went to the fridge and found he'd drunk all my beer.

So I made a cup of tea and watched the end of the film.
The zombies lost. It wasn't much like real life.

29

I was working Saturday night and Sunday daytime, so I slept in. Correction: I lay in bed looking at the ceiling and listening to the world go by outside the closed curtains. I felt about as much empathy with it as a grizzly bear does to a parking meter.

I crawled out of the pit about two. The telephone rang at three. It was Brady. He sounded well pleased with himself.

'Hello Nick,' he said. 'Top of the afternoon to ya.'

'You sound chipper,' I said.

'So would you.'

'Then I assume everything was OK with last night's little transaction.'

'You assume correctly.'

'Good kit?'

'Exactly as promised.'

'So part one of the master-plan is complete.'

'Cor-rect.'

'And part two?'

'Have some patience, Nick.'

'I want this over and done with so's I can get back to my life – what there is of it.'

'In due time.'

'So what's next?'

'I'm going to throw a party.'

'A what?'

'You heard. A party. A soirée at my place tomorrow night.'

'Who's invited?' As if I had to ask.

'Seeley and Hughes. I spoke to them this morning, and told them how delighted I was with the way things went last night. They've accepted the invitation. Jools is coming, and a few other friends of mine. Alfie will be cooking one of his chillis. He really is rather good in the kitchen department. Don't fret, dear heart, it's all a chance for us to get better acquainted. Good music, good wine and good company. And don't worry, you're on the guest list too.'

'How about our mysterious friend from last night?'

'If he wants to come.'

'That's not what I meant.'

'I know. Don't worry, we'll get round to him in time.'

'I'm sure you will.'

'You don't exactly sound ecstatic at the invitation, Nick. Got a problem with it?'

'I don't like parties,' I said.

'You'll like this one.'

'I'm not sure.'

His voice hardened. '*I* am,' he said. 'You'll be there, my friend, or I'll want to know the reason why. Nine o'clock, and don't be late.'

I hesitated and sighed down the phone. My stomach was turning over with tension, and I felt hemmed in by his voice and the four walls of the room. 'OK,' I said. 'I'll be there.'

'I knew you wouldn't find in yourself to refuse.' And he hung up. When I put down the phone, it rang again straight away. I picked up the receiver, but said nothing.

'Nick?' said a woman's voice.

'Yeah.'

'Kylie.'

'Oh, hello,' I said. Even as I did so, I could hear the flatness in the tone of my voice.

'You don't sound in a very good mood.'

'Sorry,' I said.

'Bad time?'

'When isn't?'

'If you want to leave it . . .'

I suddenly realised how pleased I was to hear her voice. 'No, not at all. I was thinking of something else. It's great to hear from you. Really.'

'I believe you, thousands wouldn't. Is that why you haven't called?'

I remembered my promise when we'd parted. 'Yeah. Sorry, babe. I've been up to here,' I said. 'You know how it is.'

'I do. That's why I rang you. What are you doing tonight?'

'Working. I'm afraid.' And I was.

'Oh.' I loved the way she said it.

'I thought you would be, too – being Saturday night and all.'

'I work when I want to. It's a perk of the job.'

'I'd like to know the others.'

'I thought you would already. What time are you through?'

'Eleven-thirty, twelve.'

'Whereabouts exactly is the place?'

'West Norwood.'

'Where the hell is that?'

'About fifteen minutes from the arse-end of the universe.'

'Sounds like it. Do cabs venture there?'

'If the passenger looks like you, they do. Otherwise it can be a bit iffy. Why, are you thinking of making the trip?'

'If the mountain won't come to Mohammed, I might. Would I be welcome?'

'As the buds in May.'

'Are you sure?'

'Absolutely.'

'Give me the address, then, and I'll see how I feel later.'

I told her. 'There's a class Indian just down the road,' I

said. 'Stays open late on a Saturday night.'

'Wow. Be still, my beating heart. For the local public-bar crowd I imagine.'

'No. The clientele is impeccable.'

'In West whatever-it-is.'

'If I didn't know better, I'd say you'd been here before.'

'Places similar. I've been around.'

'Well get around here later and I'll buy you a lager and lime.'

'A double?'

'You got it.'

'Sounds better all the time.'

'So it's a date?'

'Yeah, OK. About ten-thirty?'

'Sounds good.'

'See you, then.'

'See you.'

I let her hang up first. I haven't done that for a long time.

30

Kylie was a little late. I imagined she'd had a harder job than she thought she would getting a cab to venture this far into the black hole of south London. I swear taxi drivers think they're going to drop off the edge of the earth if they venture past Waterloo Station. Mind you, I was surprised. Looking the way she looked as she came through the door of the bar, if I'd been a cabbie I'd've volunteered to drive her to Tibet, or someplace even more remote. I suppose she arrived at JJ's at twenty to eleven or thereabouts, near closing time, and the place was Saturday-night busy. Buzzin', as you might say. But she managed to lower the volume of conversation, if not the worn-out, original 45rpm Top Rank single recording of 'Quarter to Three' by US Bonds that was booming out of the mighty Wurlitzer juke-box.

Her hair was loose, and fell to her shoulders, and it was the shade that blonde was in TV commercials for Sunsilk Shampoo. If you'd asked me, I'd've said she was wearing minimal make-up, but that was a trick. She'd just made it look that way. She was wearing black high-heeled patent-leather court shoes, black fishnets and a little black dress that she filled to within an ounce of overflowing. But it was that ounce that she and every man in the room lived in. Over one shoulder was a black leather handbag on a long strap, and over the other arm was a black cloth coat. She ignored the stares and the dropped jaws and interrupted conversations that preceded and followed her path, and made straight for me.

'Hello, Nick,' she said as the record faded into the scratchy run-out. 'Sorry I'm late.'

'It was worth it for that entrance,' I said.

She cocked a look at one of our regulars who was sitting next to her on a bar-stool. He resisted her gaze for a nanosecond before offering her his seat. Previous to that moment, I'd have doubted that he would have made the gesture to a nine-month pregnant woman whose water had just broken.

'Thanks,' she said, and perched up on the vacant seat, showing enough fishnetted thigh to give any man ideas of trawling as a career. 'So where's that drink you promised me?' she asked.

'Lager and lime, wasn't it?' I said.

She nodded, and the next record started to play. 'Pretty Flamingo' it was, by *Manfred Mann*. Perfect, I thought, and went to the fridge for a bottle of Sol.

When I fetched her the beer, with a slice of lime in the neck, I could see and feel most of the eyes of the customers in the place still on us. 'Do you always cause such a stir?' I asked, under the sound of the music.

'I try to.'

'You succeeded. My charisma count just went up a point or ten.'

'That's exactly what I wanted.'

By then the next-to-last-order merchants were clamouring to be served, so I had to leave her. As I poured drinks, I saw one or two of our likelier lads trying to put the bite on her, but she deflected them like a heavyweight boxer taking on a six-year-old.

I called last orders at eleven, and herded the reluctant punters out as quickly as drinking-up time allowed. By half-past the place was virtually empty, and JJ put in an appearance. He pulled the sort of face that people do when they want to know if the other person was someone I was involved with, and I pulled the sort of face back that said yes. He tossed me the spare keys I'd need to open up the next morning, and told us to go. I didn't need to be told twice. I helped her on with her coat and we split.

Outside she turned to me and said, 'Where's this class Indian you were telling me about then?'

'Just down the hill,' I said. 'Come on, I'll race you.'

'Not in these heels,' she replied, and attached herself to my arm and we walked down slowly.

As it goes it's not a bad Indian, as Indians go in that neck of the woods. Not exactly subtle, but not bad. And they served Kingfisher lager. Freezing cold in bottles.

When we'd got a table, I asked her what she wanted to drink and she said beer, so I ordered two, plus a stack of papadoms and the chutney tray. They don't serve the spicy tomato thing, so that was a point against them. But, as I've noted before, nothing's perfect.

When the beer had washed down a couple of the big crisps, and the most urgent hunger pangs had been sated, I said, 'I'm glad you came over. It's good to see you.'

'I thought you weren't going to ring.'

'Like I said, I've been up to here.' I put up my hand and touched the top of my head.

'Business?'

'Yeah.'

'Funny business with Roy and Pat?'

'Don't ask.'

'OK, I won't. But, Nick, be careful. Those two are no good.'

'I will. Now, can we talk about something pleasant?'

'Course. Sorry.'

'Right. We're here. *They're* not. Let's forget about them.'

So we did, and the meal was a great success.

Afterwards I drove her back to my place. It was after one in the morning by then, and she seemed in no hurry to go anywhere else, so I just rode with the flow. I let her into my flat and switched on the light.

151

'Nice,' she said. 'If a little – how can I say – cramped.'

'Bloody cramped,' I agreed. 'Even poky, runty or puny. But also compact, bijou, snug or cosy. Depends how you look at it. It suits me. Like I told you, I'm usually on my own.'

'I remember. But not tonight.'

'That's true, and is it going to be all night?'

'Of course. If you think I'm going to go out and find a cab at this hour . . .'

'You know I'd drive you home if you want.'

'But I don't want. Now I'm in Tulse Hill, I'll stay here.'

'Are you sure you haven't been here before?'

'What?' She looked confused.

'You know this is Tulse Hill.'

'You told me.'

'Did I? I thought I said West Norwood.'

'The other night. You told me you live in Tulse Hill.'

'Then I forget. Never mind. It doesn't matter. Drink?'

'Please,'

'Beer? Gin? Vodka? Jack Daniel's?'

'Jack Daniels sounds good.'

'A woman after my own heart,' I said, and got a pair of drinks together.

When I took them through from the kitchenette, she was still standing in the middle of the room, coat on, like she'd changed her mind about staying. I put the drinks down on the low table next to the sofa that converts into a bed.

'Let me take your coat,' I said. 'Sit down.'

She took it off. That dress. Boy, that dress.

She sat down demurely, pulling her skirt lower on her thighs. I sat next to her and she passed over my drink.

'Cheers,' I said.

'Cheers,' she replied, and we both drank.

'Want some music?' I asked.

'No. I like it like this. This time of night in the city. It's like it's closed down. Or maybe not that at all. It's as if you could open the curtains and just see deserted countryside for miles.' She looked embarrassed. 'Or is that silly?'

'No,' I said. 'You have a very lyrical turn of phrase.'

'But you know what I mean?'

I nodded. I did. I've walked hundreds, no, thousands of miles through the streets of London in the night-time. When the orange sodium lamps give colour to the wet streets. Not real colour. Just a veneer of colour. A sheen, like oil on black skin.

'I knew you would,' she said and came closer to me. I touched her, and the touch turned to a caress. And the caress to something else. And the something else to something else again.

We woke up in bed as close as two spoons. She smiled and I smiled, and it was great just to be there. I told her I was due to open up the bar, and we got up and took turns at the bathroom, and I made breakfast. When we'd finished eating she said, 'I forgot. I've got something for you.'

'What?' I asked.

She got up from the table and fetched her handbag. She took something out and placed it next to my plate. It was a chromed Zippo lighter.

'What's this?' I asked. Stupid question, really.

'What does it look like? You're always lighting your cigarettes with that horrible plastic throwaway thing. I saw this and bought it for you.'

'You shouldn't have.'

'Why not?'

I didn't know. 'I don't know,' I said.

'Well, there you go. Take it. It wasn't expensive.'

'Cheers. It's nice to know how much I'm worth.'

'You know I didn't mean it like that.'

'I know. I'm only teasing. But I always lose lighters.

153

That's why I use a disposable. Perhaps I should put it somewhere safe.'

'No, don't do that. Please.'

'OK, I won't,' I said, and got up from my seat and kissed her. 'Thanks. That was kind of you.' If I hadn't had to go to open up the bar, the kiss might have lasted all day. 'Sorry,' I said. 'I've got to go to work.' I looked at my watch. 'I've just got time to get you home.'

'Don't worry about that. I'll get a cab.'

'No,' I said. 'It's OK. After all, you did give me this.' I held up the lighter.

'Promise you'll use it.'

'I'll never go anywhere without it again.'

She smiled and I dropped it in my pocket, got my keys, took her down to the car and up to town.

'When am I going to see you again?' she asked.

I'd considered asking her to Brady's party, but thought better of it. I really didn't think that Kylie and Jools in the same room would be a good idea, considering.

'I'll ring you,' I said when I dropped her off in Brewer Street.

'That's what you said last time.'

'This time I will. Promise.' And I kissed her again.

The kiss lasted quite a while, but eventually she disengaged herself and got out of the car. I missed her straight away.

31

I drove straight to the bar. Being Sunday, it didn't open until twelve, and there were no deliveries, and JJ did the honours on the cleaning stakes. So it didn't matter if I didn't get there until dead on the appointed hour. The church clock opposite was striking as I pulled up, and there was already a couple of thirsty-looking customers standing outside, clutching newspapers. I sleepwalked through the day, not saying much. At six-thirty I handed over to JJ.

I went home and made a sandwich and washed it down with a glass of milk. I wasn't that hungry, but eating passed the time. I sat around until about eight, then showered and changed into a fresh shirt and a newly dry-cleaned suit straight out of its clingy film of plastic. I put a few quid into the back trouser pocket, cigarettes and lighter into the jacket, picked up the keys to the Cosworth off the table, and got on my merry way. Not that I was feeling particularly merry. I wasn't looking forward to the evening ahead at all.

I arrived outside Brady's place at nine-fifteen precisely. There were already a couple of expensive cars parked at the kerb, including a familiar-looking Jaguar XJS. Interesting. My brisk rat-a-tat-tat on the door-knocker was answered by Alfie looking adorable in a baggy rainbow-coloured shirt and black jeans.

'Do you have to knock like that?' he asked crossly.

'What do you mean?' I asked innocently.

'It has connotations.'

Connotations of Old Bill turning over some previous drum of yours, I thought. 'Sorry,' I said. 'I'll try to remember.'

'If you wouldn't mind. Well, you'd better come in.' He opened the door all the way, and closed it firmly behind me once I was inside the hall. From deeper inside the house I could hear 'Joanna' by *Kool And The Gang* on the stereo. Real hairdresser's music.

'What's it all about, Alfie?' I asked. But he didn't get it. Too young, I expect.

'There's a few people here.'

'Lead me to it,' I said.

'Straight through into the living-room,' he said. 'I've got to check the food.'

I followed the sound of music and found the party, what there was of it so far. The living-room was next to the kitchen, and also looked out on to the tiny garden at the back. The furniture was modern. All black wood, smoked glass, chrome and leather, and it had been pushed to one side and canapés had been put out on plates on top of a low unit. Enough booze, mixers, ice and glasses to stock a pub were lined up on the dining table next to the patio door, which was open a crack to let in some air.

Brady was standing talking to Pat Hughes and a mean-looking individual wearing a pink double-breasted jacket, black shirt buttoned to the neck without a tie, baggy black slacks and polished black lace-ups, with a long-legged blonde hooked on to one arm. It was the guy I'd seen a few days before coming out of the house. The one with the Jaguar XJS. If he had been playing house with Alfie that afternoon I saw him coming out of the place, and now he was with the blonde, he had to be AC/DC. As Jools had put it, he swung both ways. Interesting.

When I entered, Brady immediately abandoned the trio and came towards me, hand outstretched. 'Nick,' he said, too effusively and too loudly, and grabbed my right hand

and pumped it hard. By the sound of his voice, and the look in his eyes, he'd been at the goodies already. 'So glad to see you,' he went on. 'There's someone over here I want you to meet.'

He led me back to Hughes and the geezer in the pink jacket.

'Hello, Pat,' I said.

Hughes nodded to me. 'How are you?' he said.

'Fine,' I replied.

'And this is Gregor,' said Brady, introducing me to pink jacket, who close-up looked even meaner than he had from a distance. 'Nick, Gregor. Gregor, Nick.'

His name fitted him like a glove. Gregor raised one hand in a sort of half salute, half wave. 'Nick,' he said.

'Gregor,' I said back.

'I'm Fanny,' said the blonde, in a high-pitched, little girl's voice.

I'll just bet you are, I thought. 'Hello, Fanny,' was all I said, and smiled a neutral smile. 'It's very nice to meet you.'

'You too,' she replied, and stuck out her hand like a duchess. I didn't know if I was expected to kiss it, or what, so I just gave it a gentle squeeze.

'Gregor is cool,' said Brady. By that I assumed that Brady meant he was a villain. I think I could have worked that one out for myself. 'Let me get you a drink,' Brady continued. 'Champagne?'

'It gives me a headache,' I said. 'Got any vodka?'

'Of course. With?'

'Orange juice.'

'One screwdriver coming up.' And he went over to the table and started clinking bottles and ice and a glass together.

'Where's Roy?' I asked Hughes.

'He'll be along,' he said. As if on cue, the doorbell rang. 'That might be him now.'

A few seconds later Roy and Jools, led by Alfie, came

into the room. Roy was wearing an very expensive-looking pinstriped suit, and Jools wore a little black dress that showed off the tops of her breasts to perfection, and strappy high-heeled shoes. She was carrying a tiny black velvet evening-bag in one hand. Brady gave me my drink and be-bopped over to welcome them.

'Hello, you two,' he said. 'Glad you could make it.'

'Hi,' said Roy, who looked like he'd snorted half of Bolivia before coming out to play, and appeared somewhat the worse for wear for it.

'Let me get you something to drink,' said Brady. 'Champagne?' There it was again. The worst alcoholic drink ever invented by man, wheeled out like it was a big deal.

'Yeah,' said Seeley. 'But I've got something better in me sky rocket.'

'Groovy,' said Brady, like a schoolboy who'd just heard that gobstoppers had come off the ration. He went over to the table and poured two glasses of champagne, and gave one each to Seeley and Jools, then dragged them over and introduced them to Gregor and Fanny. After the introductions were complete, they excused themselves and made for the food.

Then Seeley came and buttonholed me. 'Hi, Nick,' he said. 'Listen, I've got some business to talk with Brady and Pat. Look after Jools for me for a minute. We won't be long.' He winked. 'Don't worry, I'll look after you later.'

I knew just what business he was on about. 'No problem,' I replied.

He went over to Brady and whispered in his ear. I saw Brady nod in affirmation, and Seeley tapped Hughes on the shoulder, and the three of them left the room together. Seeley took the bottle of champagne with him. They passed Alfie at the door, who gave Brady a dirty look and then waltzed over to Gregor and Fanny to check how the food was going.

158

'Seems like I'm always being left to look after you,' I said to Jools.

'The booby prize,' she said, but she didn't specify which one of us was the booby. 'This looks like being a riotous affair,' she went on.

'A real jolly up,' I agreed.

The front-door bell rang again, and Alfie broke off his conversation to answer it. He reappeared with a pair of junior hitmen for the mob dressed in sharp navy-blue suits, white shirts and narrow black ties.

'Who's this?' said Jools. 'The Blues Brothers?'

'In their dreams,' I said. 'Want another drink?'

'Yeah, and something to eat.' We got re-fills and wandered over to the canapés, and I held both glasses whilst she loaded two plates. The food wasn't bad, as it goes. Either Alfie was as good a cook as Brady had said, or else he had a charge card at Harrods. There was six different kind of smoked meat, prawns and caviar with slices of hard-boiled egg, lobster vol-au-vents and pâté.

'Very nice,' I said through a mouthful.

'A bit like a tart's tea party,' said Jools. 'But not bad.'

When we'd finished she said, 'I'd better go and find Roy – see what state he's in.'

'OK,' I replied. 'I'll mingle.'

By that time a few more faces had shown up. A couple of the blokes had young women in tow. Good-looking they were, too. But strictly property to be bought and sold like meat on a rack. There were a few men on their own, too, or in pairs, like the Blues Brothers, but nothing overtly gay. Nothing that would upset the sensibilities of the real hard-men present.

As I circulated, I got snatches of the conversations. You know the sort of thing: houses, cars, clothes, holidays. I didn't mingle. Just drifted. Nobody paid me much attention and that was just the way I liked it.

32

Eventually, as I drifted round, I got back into Gregor's sphere of influence.

'Nick,' he said, when I got close. 'Come and talk to me. We didn't have a chance earlier.' He was standing in the darkest corner of the room, furthest from the door, drink in one hand, long-legged blonde still attached to the other arm like a successful transplant. As I moved in closer, she fixed me with an unblinking stare from her wide blue eyes. 'You remember Fanny don't you?' he asked.

How could I forget? 'Of course,' I said.

'So what do you do, Nick?'

'I work behind the bar in a restaurant.'

'Really. I'm in the restaurant game myself.'

'Is that so?'

'Sure. I own half a dozen nice places round Lewisham, Blackheath – that part of town. But they're just a sideline.' He winked and moved closer to me, dragging Fanny like a sheet anchor. 'I make my real money in other ways. You're a friend of Brady's. You know what I'm talking about.'

'Sure,' I said.

'Nothing *too* heavy. Just a few fingers in a few pies.'

'Sure,' I said again.

'Maybe you and I could do something. Any friend of Brady's . . . You know what I mean. You must pay us a visit. Pop over and have a meal with me. Best in the house. Anything you want is yours.'

'I'd like that,' I said.

'We'll fix it up. Soon. Call me.' He unhooked Fanny and fished in his jacket pocket and came up with a pasteboard card. 'My office number,' he said. 'Any time. Bring someone with you. We'll make up a foursome. Just ask for me. I'm always around.'

'Sounds good,' I said, and glanced at the card. The address was in Greenwich. I stuck it in my breast pocket.

Gregor re-attached Fanny like an intravenous drip, then something caught his eye behind me. 'I think your friend is looking for you,' he said.

I looked over my shoulder. Jools was standing in the doorway. When she caught sight of me she waved half-heartedly.

'I'd better go see what she wants,' I said.

'Sure. I'll catch you later.'

'You got it.' I left the pair and went across the room.

When I got close to Jools I could see she looked stressed out. 'What's up?' I asked.

'It's Roy. He's being a pain.'

'What's the matter?'

'Too much coke. He's been at it all day. And now the booze on top. He can be such an arsehole sometimes. Now he wants to see you. He wants you to have some. Come and help calm him down? He won't listen to any of us. He's already picked a fight with Pat, and *he* went before it got serious. Roy's impossible when he's like this. Brady's worried he's going to ruin the party.'

'I don't know what I can do,' I said.

'Anything. Just try. He's upstairs.'

I followed her up a single flight and into what I assumed was the master bedroom. It was decorated in pastel shades and softly lit. A right passion palace. I'd bet Brady and Alfie got up to some performances in the massive double bed covered by a flower-patterned duvet. Seeley was sitting at a dark wood, glass-topped dressing-table, cutting out huge lines from a mountain of coke next to the empty

162

bottle of champagne he'd liberated from the living-room downstairs. Brady was standing beside him looking well pissed off.

'Nick,' said Seeley when we walked in. 'I see the jailer found you.' I looked at Jools, but she just shrugged. 'That cunt's no fun anymore. She just wants to stop me having any. Come and get it, mate. There's plenty here for my friends.' If anything, he was looking worse than when he'd arrived. The top button of his shirt was undone and his tie had been pulled loose, and the skin on his face was grey and slack and sweaty-looking.

'What's up, Roy?' I asked.

'Nothing's up. Who said it was?' He looked accusingly at Jools. 'That fucking cow, I suppose.'

I ignored him. 'Having a good time?' I asked.

'Fucking awful. Everybody's being a drag. But now you're here it's going to get better. Take a fucking line and cool out.' He brushed two hundred quid's worth of charlie on to the carpet with the sleeve of his jacket as he gestured towards the table top, and he thrust a rolled-up bank note towards me. I sat down next to him on the edge of the stool and snorted up a line. 'Good man, Nick,' he slurred. 'I knew you wouldn't let me down. You're from the old school. I recognised that the first time I talked to you.' Now he was getting maudlin. There's nothing worse. 'Have some more,' he urged.

'Not now, Roy,' I said. 'I've had enough.'

'There's never enough. Never enough of anything.' He leant over and put his arm round my shoulder. 'Except fucking nagging fucking women. Isn't that right?'

'I don't know, mate,' I replied, gently disentangling myself. 'I don't know any.'

'You're lucky.'

'Why don't you have a little lie-down,' I said.

'Lie-down. Why?'

'You're out of it. The rest'll do you good.'

'Am I? Will it?'

'Yeah. Come on I'll help you,' I said, and stood up, and helped him to his feet. He was high as a kite and pissed up, and he didn't resist as I led him over to the bed, and helped him off with his jacket and he lay down. With any luck he'd pass out and remember nothing when he came to. 'Take off his shoes,' I said to Jools.

She did as she was told, and he sighed. 'That feels good,' he said. 'You're a mate, Nick. Now, look after my darling for me.'

I looked at Jools again, and she shrugged once more, as if it was par for the course for him to hate her one minute, love her the next.

'I'll do that,' I said. 'See you later.'

'Later,' he replied. And I herded everyone outside on to the landing and closed the door behind us.

'Well done, Nick,' said Brady.

'No big deal,' I said. 'I'm sure you could have handled it yourself.'

'I didn't want to knock him out, did I? Pat had to split before he did. Roy was calling him every slag under the sun.'

'He gets like that,' said Jools.'

'Sorry he was rough on you,' I said.

'Forget it, I'm used to it,' she replied.

'He'll sleep it off with any luck,' I said. 'But we'd better check on him every so often.'

The other two nodded, and we went downstairs to rejoin the party. 'I need a drink,' I said.

'Me too,' said Jools, and we made for the booze supply. I poured a vodka for myself, and Jools asked for a scotch. Alfie had cleared away the canapés and laid out a big pot of chilli, another of rice, a tray of pitta bread and a bowl of salad.

'Hungry?' I asked.

'Not just now. Maybe later.'

'Suits me,' I said. We stood and drank and chatted for half an hour or so, as the rest of the party circulated round us. Then she decided she wanted something to eat, and of course the chilli bowl was empty.

'There's a pot on the stove,' said Alfie. 'Help yourself.' So I collected Jools and took her into the kitchen, and that was where Seeley found us, alone. He was still looking rough, but maybe a little better. He'd put on his shoes and jacket, and adopted another bottle of champagne which he was drinking from the neck.

'What's going on?' he demanded.

'Just having something to eat and talking,' said Jools.

'Make sure that's all it is,' he said.

'Slow down,' I said. 'You heard what she said.'

'Who asked you?' he said nastily.

'You did,' I said. 'You asked me to look after her.'

'You *did*, Roy,' said Jools. 'Twice.'

'Shut up, you slag,' he said.

'Oh, Roy, don't start again. I can't stand it.'

He put his face up close to hers. I could see the foam in the corners of his mouth, and the flecks of flying spittle as he spoke. 'I said shut up, you slag,' he said very slowly.

'Back off, Roy,' I said. 'Cool down, mate. Take it easy. Everything's all right.'

He poked the bottle into my chest. 'Don't tell me. I've found her "just talking" before. But usually she's got her knickers round her ankles while she's doing it.'

Jools lifted up first one foot, then the other, and studiously looked at them. 'Not this time, Roy,' she said. 'And even if they were, it's none of your fucking business. Anyway, it's been such a long time since you've shown any interest in my knickers that I'd be surprised if you'd recognise a pair if you saw them. Unless you were wearing them yourself, of course.'

He hit her then. An open-handed slap around the face

with all his strength behind it, that knocked her head sideways.

So I hit him. Right on the nose, where even a light blow can cause much pain, distress, and even tears. The works. And, believe me, it wasn't a light blow. He went backwards across the kitchen, hit the oven and crashed to the floor, dropping the champagne bottle but acquiring the pan of hot chilli all over his suit in the process.

Jools looked down at him, and touched her cheek, which was already beginning to swell up. 'I wish you hadn't done that,' she said. 'I'll be paying it back for months.'

I leaned over him and found two reasonably chilli-free zones on the lapels of his jacket, and hauled him to his feet. 'If I hear,' I said, as slowly as he'd spoken to her, 'that you've touched her because of what I did, I'll do it again. And again, until you stop. Understand?'

He looked at me with an expression that said I had made a *bad* enemy.

I let go of his lapels and pushed him away. '*Understand*?' I asked again.

He nodded. But I knew he was already thinking of ways to get even.

'Now go and clean yourself up,' I said.

He looked down at his ruined clothes, and then at me, and then at Jools. He left the kitchen without a word.

Jools sighed and followed him.

Twenty seconds later Alfie swished in and looked at the wreckage of the kitchen. 'Sorry,' I said. 'It was an accident.'

'You didn't intend to hit him, you mean?'

'I meant to hit him all right. But I didn't mean for *him* to hit the main course.'

'Typical,' said Alfie sniffily, and found a mop and bucket and started cleaning up.

Twenty seconds after that, Brady arrived on the scene. 'What the fuck did you do that for?' he demanded.

Everybody who came into the kitchen seemed to be full of questions.

'He asked for it,' I said.

'He's our contact.'

'He's *your* contact. And he was too fisty with her.'

'So who died and made you a knight in shining armour? It's none of your fucking business what he does with her. Fucking stupid bitch probably asked for it. This is just what I *didn't* want to happen. You've probably blown it, son. That's what you've done.'

Alfie was listening hard throughout our brief conversation.

'And what are you going to do with her now?' asked Brady.

'Nothing. What am I supposed to do with her? We were only talking.'

'Oh,' he said, drawing it out like you would if you were talking to someone a little slow on the uptake. 'Are you stupid or what? I bet she knew that talking to you would get him at it – state he was in. You mug.'

'Bollocks,' I said. 'He asked me to take care of her. Then he went on the bloody turn when I did. His fucking brain's gone. Too much booze and coke. Where is he? I'll sort him out.'

'Not tonight you won't. He's hopped it.'

'What?'

'You heard. Hopped it. Left. Fucked off in his motor. Get my drift?'

'Oh shit.'

'Oh shit is right. You started it. You finish it. I've got to sort him out tomorrow. We've got a deal on, remember?'

At that juncture Jools came back into the kitchen. 'He's gone,' she said.

'So I believe,' I replied.

'So I'm with *you* now.'

'What?'

'You heard.'

'Hold on. He's your bloke. Go home and make up. I'll call you a cab.'

'What fucking planet do you come from?' she demanded. 'He's not my bloke, as you so nicely put it. He hasn't been for months. You saw the way he was tonight. And if you think I'm going round there on me tod tonight to get a good kicking from that bastard, because you hit him, you'd better think again. You're the one who done him. It's down to you.' Her accent was moving freely from the West to the East End the more agitated she got.

It reminded me of that old old Chinese tradition that if you save a person's life you are ever after responsible for them. In other words I was lumbered.

'OK,' I said. 'So it's down to me. I'll sort it. We'd better go.'

'Where?'

'I don't know. We'll talk about it in the car.'

33

It was all quiet outside, with no sign of Seeley's car anywhere. Jools and I climbed into mine and she asked for a cigarette. I gave her one and lit it. 'So?' I said. 'Where to?'

'Don't ask me.'

'Haven't you got any friends you can stay with?'

She shook her head, and her white hair gleamed in the light from the street-lamps.

'Got any money for a hotel?'

'I haven't got a penny. And I'm not staying in some flea-bag round here, thank you. Don't think you can just drop me off somewhere and forget about me.'

She was getting to be more of a nuisance by the minute. 'Looks like it's my place, then,' I said.

'Looks like it,' she replied.

I switched on the engine and lights, put the car into first, and drove slowly out of the cul-de-sac and headed south. 'He knows where I live,' I said.

'Is that supposed to make me feel better,' she asked.

'It's not supposed to make you feel anything. It's a fact. If he decides to come looking . . .' I didn't finish the sentence.

'I doubt it,' she said. 'State he was in.'

When we got into my street I switched off the main beams and drove slowly past my house, checking for Seeley's car. It wasn't about. I did a three-point turn and drove back. 'You're being careful, aren't you?' she said.

'Always,' I replied. 'I like to know what I'm walking into.'

I parked the car up on the front, and let us in. She followed me up the stairs and we went into the flat together. 'Not much of a place, is it?' she said. She wasn't as polite as Kylie had been, and I wished it was Kylie I was coming in with, instead of the miserable bitch I was with. I didn't bother to try and defend the place, or even point out that beggars can't be choosers. It would just have been a waste of breath, the mood she was in.

'Home sweet home for the night,' was all I said.

'And the rest.'

I let that one pass, too.

'You can have the bed,' I said. 'I'll take the sofa.'

'The perfect gentleman,' she said.

'That's me.' I turned on the bedside lamp and switched off the main light. 'Coffee?' I asked.

'Sure. Why not?' I went and put the kettle on, and sorted out the spare duvet and a pillow, and made up the sofa into a bed.

She watched me all the while. 'You don't have to do that, you know,' she said. 'You can sleep with me. I haven't got the clap.'

It wasn't exactly an enticing thought, and, even if it had been, it wasn't on. Something about the picture wasn't right.

'I never thought you had,' I said. 'I just don't think it's a very good idea.'

'Why not? You scared of me?'

'No,' I said. 'I just don't think it's a very good idea, that's all.'

She sniffed. It's just like asking for credit in a boozer. A refusal often offends.

When I'd finished with the sofa, I made the coffees, and she sat on the edge of her bed and I sat on the edge of mine whilst we drank them. In fact we were almost knee to knee. It was quiet as we sat there facing each other, and the room was electric with tension. When we finished, I put the cups into the sink, and she stood up and pulled her dress over her head and tossed it across the bed. All she had on underneath was a pair of brief black panties. No bra. No stockings or tights. I've got to tell you she was well fit, and I almost regretted my decision to sleep alone. Almost but not quite.

She looked at me looking at her. 'Do you approve?' she asked. 'Up to scratch, or what?'

'No complaints,' I said.

'And you still don't want to sleep with me?'

I shook my head.

'Are you sure you're not a faggot, like your friend?'

'Sure,' I said.

You could have fooled me,' she said scornfully.

I ignored that comment, too, and she climbed in to the bed. I undressed down to my boxers and T-shirt, and got under the duvet on the sofa.

'Shall I switch off the light or are you frightened of the dark, too?' she asked.

Once again I didn't take the bait. 'Turn it off,' I said.

She did, and flung herself around under the sheets, and sighed like people do when they want a fuck and can't get one – and want whoever else is there to *know* they want one. Christ, I've done it myself enough times. It's a right bastard of a feeling, as it goes. I was tempted to get out of my bed and into hers, and give her what she wanted, just to shut her up. But I thought better of it, and just lay there and let her get on with it. Eventually she quietened down and her breathing evened out, and I guessed she was asleep. I toyed with the idea of getting the Howdah pistol down from the loft just in case Seeley paid a dawn visit. But before I could make a decision I was asleep myself.

34

When I woke up, Jools was still asleep. I got off the sofa and went into the bathroom. When I came back she was awake.

'I thought you'd run out on me,' she said.

'No,' I replied. 'Coffee?'

'Please.'

I put the kettle on and washed up last night's cups.

'Have you got a dressing-gown?' she asked. She wasn't quite as bold in the cold light of dawn – or at 8.40 am as in fact it was – as she had been the previous night.

'Sure,' I said, and got my robe off the back of the bathroom door and tossed it to her. 'I won't look,' I said. I fiddled about, putting the coffee in the cups, as she got out of bed and brushed past me on the way to the bathroom. 'There's a new toothbrush in the cabinet,' I said. By the time she emerged, the coffee was ready. 'Want something to eat?' I asked.

She shook her head.

'Are you sure? I'm having some toast.'

'No thanks. I don't eat in the morning.'

'Please yourself.'

I put a couple of slices of bread under the grill, and dug out the butter and a pot of marmalade. She sat at the breakfast bar and watched me over the rim of her cup as I prepared the food.

'Have you always lived alone?' she asked.

'No,' I replied. 'I was married once. I'm divorced now.'

I seemed to keep having the same conversation with people. But life's like that. You don't talk about something for months, and then all of a sudden it's the prime subject on the agenda.

'I'm sorry about all the cracks last night,' she said. 'I was uptight. It really wasn't your fault you got involved. It was that fucking Roy. He's a crazy bastard.'

'Do you think he'll come looking for you.'

'I don't know. I doubt it. A couple of years ago, yes. But I'm too old for him now, and too wise. He'll have an eighteen-year-old bimbo on his arm by the end of the week, I expect. Not that he hasn't had plenty of them already, as you know. But he won't forget that you hit him. Be careful, Nick. He won't forget that you hit him and went off with me. He'll never believe we slept in separate beds. Not in a million years. Even though he doesn't want me himself, he won't want anyone else to have me.'

'What do you think he'll do?'

'He won't do anything. He's not into that – violence. He doesn't mind knocking me about a bit, but he won't take on a man. He's too scared he might get hit back. He'll go to Pat. Pat'll do it for him. Watch out for him, Nick. He's a wicked bastard. He . . .' She stopped.

'What?' I asked.

'Nothing. It doesn't matter. Just be careful.'

'Meanwhile?' I asked.

'Meanwhile you've got yourself a slightly used lodger. Mind if I stick around? I can cook, clean, wash, iron. The works. What do you say?'

'I don't think so.'

'Why not?'

I didn't answer.

Then it dawned on her. 'Is there someone else?'

'Sort of.'

'Who?'

'Just someone I met recently.'

'Why wasn't she with you last night?'

'It's a long story,' I said.

'Is it serious?'

I shrugged. 'Who knows?'

'Then what does it matter? You can go about with who you like. I'm used to it, Nick. It doesn't make any difference if it's you or him that's doing it.'

'I don't want to do it that way.'

She was silent for a moment. 'I'll go then,' she said.

I felt like a right bastard. Even though I didn't want her to stay, I didn't want to kick her out. Whatever the reason, it had been *me* who whacked Seeley. 'There's no rush,' I said. 'Get yourself together first. Find somewhere to stay.'

'OK, Nick. Thanks. But there is one thing.'

'What?'

'Have you got any money?'

'Some. Why?' A naive question.

'Because I can't go far in that dress and those shoes.'

'What about your own stuff, at your place?'

'It looks like I don't have a place anymore. He'll probably rip up my clothes, or burn them or something. Anyway, I don't want to go there.'

'I'll go for you. Got the keys?'

'Sure. But I don't know about you going in there. That'll get him really mad.'

'I'll risk it,' I said.

She considered it. 'Give it a couple of days,' she said. 'Maybe the weekend would be best.'

'OK,' I said.

'Meanwhile I'll need some cash.'

'How much?'

'Five hundred.'

'*How much*?'

'I've got nothing, remember. Just the bit of make-up I've got in my bag. No clothes except what I stand up in,

175

and you know there's not much of them. No Tampax, and I can feel my period coming on. No nothing. Just myself.' The way she said it made me think she didn't consider that much of a bargain, and I felt like a bastard again.

I thought about the cash that Endesleigh had sent to me via Brady. 'OK,' I said 'Five hundred it is. No problem.'

'I'll pay you back.'

'Don't worry about it.'

'OK, Nick. Thanks. I'm really grateful.'

35

We sat around drinking coffee and not saying much for a couple of hours. There didn't seem to be much to say. The telephone rang at about eleven. It was Brady. He didn't waste any time on niceties. Just cut straight to the plot. 'Is she there with you?' he asked.

I didn't have to ask who he meant. 'Yes,' I said.

'Can she hear what I'm saying?'

'No,' I replied.

'She'd better not be able to. You've done your best to screw this up good and proper, haven't you?'

'Look . . .' I tried to interrupt.

'Shut up,' he said. 'Shut up right now. What was the idea of that stunt last night?'

'You know very well. I wasn't going to stand by and watch him get off knocking her about.'

Jools stiffened, and looked over at me. I tried to give her a reassuring smile. From the look on her face I don't think it came out right. That wasn't surprising. I didn't feel very reassuring just then.

'It was none of your business. I already told you that,' he said.

'Bollocks,' I said. 'I made it my business.'

'And you fucked up *my* business in the process.'

I didn't say that it seemed pretty fucked up already.

'So what are you going to do with her?' he asked.

'God knows,' I said. 'What can I do?'

'Fuck her,' said Brady. 'But then I expect you already

have. I hope it was worth it.'

'As a matter of fact you're wrong.'

'Jesus wept. I was right. You do think you're a knight in shining armour, don't you? Listen, I've got news for you, pal. They're extinct. And if you're not careful, you'll be joining them.'

'I take it you've spoken to Seeley.' I saw Jools stiffen in her seat again.

'Sure I have. And I can tell you you're right at the top of his shit-list.'

'Oh dear. I can hardly hold the phone I'm trembling so.'

'Listen, Sharman, you arsehole, I had to do some fast talking to stop him sending Hughes and a couple of his mates round to sort you out this morning. They were going to kill you and stripe her so's even her mother wouldn't recognise her.'

That shut me up for a moment. 'Thanks,' I said eventually. 'I owe you one.'

'More than one, I'd say.'

'But it's all going to be taken care of, isn't it?' I meant when Seeley and Hughes were arrested. But obviously I couldn't say anything with Jools there.

'Maybe. Maybe not.' He knew what I meant.

'Has it all fallen through, then?'

'No. No thanks to you and her. But they don't want you anywhere near it.'

'So?'

'So I have to do the buy.'

'That's no problem, is it? They know you now.'

'It wasn't the plan.'

'Plans are made to be changed.'

'Not my guv'nor's plans. He's another one who's not best pleased with you.'

'What's he going to do?'

'I don't know. He doesn't tell me everything. But he's

going to do something. Count on it. Maybe not now, but he's a very patient man.'

'So I'm out of it?' I said.

'For now. But don't think you made a smart move clobbering Seeley. Don't think we're going to forget you. You haven't heard the last of us, I promise.'

I didn't think I had for a moment. 'I'll bear that in mind,' I said. 'And I appreciate you doing the other thing: keeping Hughes off my back. You didn't have to.'

'I know.'

'So why did you?'

'Despite it all, I quite like you.'

'Is that right?'

'Not like that, you prat. Though it would be a shame to let him spoil that handsome face of yours.'

'Cheers,' I said. 'I mean it. Really.'

'It's all right. Now, like I say, I don't think they'll do anything until after the deal's done. They know we're mates, and they won't take a chance on fucking it up by getting me upset. They're too scared of their bosses for that. But be careful. Anything's possible.'

'So when is it going down?' I asked.

'Christ knows. You know what they're like from the last time. Even I don't know that.'

I suddenly got a terrible premonition of danger. But not because of the threats against me and Jools. The feeling sat in my stomach like a cold, leaden weight. 'Listen,' I said, 'Why don't you drop the whole thing. Leave it. There's something not right.'

'Talk sense, Nick. It's too big for that. Besides, you know it's not down to me. I'm like you, just a pawn in the game.'

I knew he was right, of course. But that didn't make it better. 'Listen,' I said, 'if there's anything I can do.'

'Haven't you done enough already?'

'I mean it.'

'Like what?'

'Like I don't know.'

'Blimey. I *was* right. You do think you're a white knight don't you? First her. Now me. Do you help old ladies across the road, too?'

I didn't answer.

'Forget it. Just keep your head down. And take my advice, get rid of that bitch.'

I ignored the comment about Jools. 'Brady, I mean it,' I said. 'I've got a funny feeling about this.' Almost pleading.

'You and me both. But what can I do?'

I knew it was no good to argue. So I left it. 'Stay in touch,' I said.

'Count on it. Who knows, I might even end up giving evidence at your trial.' And he hung up.

36

'What was that all about?' asked Jools when I came off the phone. 'As if I didn't know.'

'It was Brady.'

'I gathered that. And?'

'And apparently your boyfriend's put the heavy mob on to me.' And you, I thought. But I didn't say it.

She looked scared and glanced at the door. 'Are they coming here?'

'Not right now. There's other unfinished business first.'

'The drugs you were buying?'

'Not me. I was just the messenger boy. But I've been kicked into touch. Not flavour of the month no more. Not since I punched your boyfriend in the head.'

'I wish you'd stop calling him my boyfriend.'

'Sorry,' I said. '*Mr* Seeley.'

'So who is?'

'What?'

'Flavour of the month.'

'Brady.' I looked at her. 'Jools,' I said, 'tell me something. You were with those two after we'd met. Was anything said about a double-cross?'

She shook her head. 'No. They're straight. As straight as anyone is in that business.'

'That's reassuring,' I said.

'So what are we going to do?' she asked.

We? I thought. 'Nothing, just now. Roll with the flow. We've got a bit of time yet. At least I hope we have. Do you know when the buy's going down?'

She shook her head. 'They never told me a thing. I was just Roy's bit of skirt as far as they were concerned.'

'But not anymore.'

'No. Not anymore. I'm never going to be anyone's bit of skirt again.'

'That's good,' I said. 'Hold that thought.'

I went and made more coffee, and she paced the floor between the bed and the sofa. 'Jesus,' she said, 'but this is making me nervous.'

'What do you want to do?' I asked.

'Get out of here.'

'And go where? I thought you wanted to stay.'

'I did. But now I'm not so sure.'

'So go,' I said.

'Can I have that money?' she asked.

'Sure,' I said. 'Stay here.' I went out of the flat, closing the door behind me and went to my hidey-hole in the roof. I checked that the Howdah pistol was still there, then got out the grand that Brady had given me, split off half, replaced the rest, took the monkey back to the flat, and gave it to her.

'Thanks,' she said. 'I *will* pay you back.'

'Whenever,' I said.

'Listen,' she said, 'I've got to go.'

'That's up to you. Do you want a lift anywhere?'

'Can you take me to Fulham? I've got some friends there.'

'Sure,' I said.

She stuffed the money into her handbag and we went down to the car. As I drove to Fulham she kept looking over her shoulder at the traffic behind.

'We're not being followed,' I said.

She smiled weakly. 'I'm sorry I've brought you all this trouble, Nick. I'll make it up to you someday, I promise.'

'Don't worry about it,' I said.

She got me to drop her off in a side turning near the Broadway. She waved once, then vanished into an alley, and I turned the car round and headed home.

37

So that was Monday. I was supposed to work the evening shift, but I called in sick. I didn't want to be around the bar with Seeley and Hughes looking for a spot of revenge, no matter what Brady had said. I didn't trust them not to send around a couple of heavy lumps to sort me out. At least at home I could lock the door and I had the Howdah pistol, if nothing else.

I called Kylie, just to hear her friendly voice, but there was no answer from her number all day.

I didn't go to bed at all on Monday night, just dozed, fully dressed on the sofa with the gun by my hand. No one rang, wrote or called.

Tuesday was the same. It was my official day off, so I didn't even have to lie to JJ. I didn't go out. Just washed and shaved and changed my clothes and ate what was in the fridge. I tried Kylie again several times, but again there was no answer.

At seven the phone rang. It was Brady. 'It's on,' he said. 'Just thought I'd let you know.'

'Where . . . when?'

'Soon. Maybe tonight, maybe tomorrow. Who knows? I've got the money. They're going to let me know the details later. Like the last time.'

'Are you happy with that?'

'I've got no choice. That's the way they want it.'

'And you're covered?'

'Sure I am.'

'So when you're doing the deal, the cavalry arrive and take them down.'

'That's the plan.'

'I hope it works.'

'It's not your problem now, is it?'

'I'm not so sure.' The dread premonition that I'd been feeling since we'd last spoken came back stronger than ever. 'Brady,' I said. 'I've never liked this thing from the beginning. You be careful, d'y'hear?'

'Relax, Nick.' He changed the subject. 'How's Jools?'

'Gone,' I replied.

'Good job.'

I changed the subject back. 'Brady, listen, can't I come with you?'

'Don't be silly. If they see you, it will get blown.'

'I could hide in the back of the car. Keep out of sight.'

'You've been watching too many old movies.'

'It could work,' I urged. 'At least you wouldn't be on your own.'

'Don't be fucking stupid. I'm not going to be on my own.' And he hung up. When I rang back, his portable had been turned off and there was no answer from his home phone.

That night I sat up again. The phone rang about four. I was sitting drinking coffee and watching Donahue on TV. The programme was all about alcoholism and drug abuse. I felt quite at home with the subject matter. I turned down the sound with the remote, and answered on the second ring.

I heard a sound like a snore, or a cough. A bad cough. Terminal. 'Hello,' I said.

'Nick?' The voice was far away. Too far.

'Brady?' I said.

'Nick, that you?'

'Yes, course it is. What's happening?'

'They were here.'

'Who? What are you talking about?'

'Don't know who. Four of them. And, Nick . . .'

'Yes.'

'Alfie was here. They've got Alfie.'

'What happened?' Although I knew – and I knew I was just wasting time by asking. Too much time. Too much of his precious time.

'They had guns.'

'Are you hurt?' Stupid, stupid question.

'Bad, Nick.'

'Where are you?'

'Elephant. At the back of the shopping centre. Next to the station. In a car-park or something. Jesus, Nick, it hurts.' His voice broke, and I heard him gasping for breath.

'Have you called an ambulance?'

'Too late, Nick. Far too late.'

'Brady. Put down the phone and call an ambulance.'

'Nick, you've got to help me. Help Alfie.'

'What the hell can I do?'

'Find him. Make sure he's safe.'

'That's not my job. Tell the police. Get off the line and I'll call them.'

'No, Nick. They won't care about him. He's gay and black, and he won't have me to protect him any more.'

I hardly thought it was the time and place to discuss civil rights. 'Brady, this is crazy . . .'

'You owe me one, remember. You said so.'

'I remember.'

'I'm calling in the debt. Help him.'

'I will. But call an ambulance. Now, Brady.'

But there was nothing but silence at the other end of the connection. 'Brady,' I said, 'can you hear me?'

But all I heard was another half cough, half snore and a crash as the phone hit something hard. 'Brady!' I shouted, as if it would help – but I knew it wouldn't.

I put down the phone. Then picked it up again. But the connection was still complete, and all I got was more silence. Terrific. Just what I needed. The first copper on the scene with any sense had a hot-line right through to my phone. I slammed the receiver down again, grabbed my jacket, and left.

I made it to the Elephant in ten minutes, breaking every traffic law in the book as I went. As I drove, my head was spinning with questions I couldn't answer. Who the hell had burst in on Brady when the deal was going down? And why was Alfie with them? What was all that about? Had it been a double-cross by Seeley and Hughes, or had someone else muscled in? And where the hell had Endesleigh and his posse been whilst it was all going off? Or were they there? Christ, that was an ugly thought. How many bodies was I going to find when I got there? And who the hell else had known about the deal? Apart from me, that is.

Oh shit. Not the most pleasant thought I've ever had.

By the time I turned the Ford into the back streets behind the Elephant and Castle BR station, I hadn't answered question one.

I cruised round slowly, looking for signs of police, but the streets were quiet and deserted, and there were few lights in the flats across the open ground next to the railway. Then I saw the BMW I'd been taken in to the warehouse in London Bridge, parked up round by the railway arches, with its side-lights on. I stopped the Cosworth behind it, switched off the engine, and got out to take a look. The big saloon was empty.

Then I looked round for the place Brady had described, and it wasn't hard to find. It was one of the loading bays for the shopping centre. The metal accordion doors had been pulled back, and when I looked closer I saw that the locks had been busted open. The entrance yawned in front of me, and then a ramp dropped away, dimly lit by low-wattage lamps mounted behind metal grilles high on the walls.

38

Walking down the ramp was like a descent into hell. Not the hell of eternal fire and the screams of the damned in torment, but a chill hell that was silent except for the sound of cold drops of water dripping from the cracks in the stressed concrete ceiling, and splashing into deep black puddles that teemed with the transparent, sightless creatures that swam and crawled there, and ate each other and themselves in the constant battle for survival. A bit like human beings, I suppose. But, then, that's one for the philosophers – and I've never been a philosopher. The puddles stank of bad fish as I walked through them, but as I reached the parking area at the bottom of the ramp, the smell changed to that of cordite and used gunpowder, and that coppery stink that stuck in the back of my throat as if I'd been sucking on an old penny, and made me want to retch.

Brady's Porsche was sitting in the middle of the empty bay, headlights on. Their light splashed against the walls rich with graffiti, and created shadows black as ink across the floor. Wreathed in the light was the faint memory of smoke, like a dream that refuses to leave the corners of your mind at the coming of the morning sun. And in the reflection of the light I saw the bodies and the blood. So much blood. Oh Christ, if I live forever I'll never forget the sight of all that blood. Long streaks of it obscuring the paint sprayed on the walls. Puddles of it next to the car, and more on the car itself. Its bodywork splattered and

191

stained with viscous streaks and spots like a bad paint job that had smeared to the colour of shit in the air. And, amidst all the blood, the bodies. Sprawled like mannequins in a window display out of your worst nightmare. I checked each one for signs of life, but found none. Their wounds were horrendous. Great rips and tears and holes in their flesh. Christ knows who had killed who. Endesleigh had been smashed apart by a shotgun blast that had blown him nearly in half. Chiltern's torso had been riddled with heavy-calibre bullets that had gone right through him and torn the back of his leather jacket to shreds. Ollie, the driver of the BMW, had bled to death from a groin wound, and lay face upwards in a lake of blood that was already beginning to crust over like fondue icing on a chocolate cake.

Seeley had been shot in the back of the head, executioner-style, and his face was almost unrecognisable. It was a rust-coloured mask, and his open mouth was full of a clot of dark-coloured matter that I didn't want to think about. Hughes looked like he'd been cut down whilst trying to escape towards a door with a pale green EXIT sign above it. His back had been opened up so that I could see the white splinters of his spine and ribs embedded in the flesh of his lungs. The hard-looking face I'd met at the electronics factory with Seeley and Hughes was curled in a foetal position half under the body of the Porsche. I could see no visible wounds, but when I felt for a pulse, his skin was cool, and I couldn't find even a flutter.

That was six of them. Then I went looking for Brady. The driver's door of the Porsche was open, and he had bled to death over the leather upholstery. His face was the colour of raw chicken skin, and his eyes were open and staring through the blood-flecked windscreen. The car-phone receiver was clutched in a death grip in his right hand. I closed his eyes for him and tried to prise the phone out of his hand. His fingers had set around the plastic like steel talons, and I snapped one with a sound like a gun being cocked and I jumped at the noise, like a schoolgirl being touched up for the first time. Eventually I got the receiver free, and reached over and tore the whole phone fitment out of the centre console.

As I stepped away from the car, I looked around again. Something was not quite right with the picture. Then I realised. There was no sign of any bags of money or drugs. And no weapons. Someone had done a thorough clean-up job. Just in case, I checked the back seat and the boot of the Porsche. Nothing. Whoever had done the killing had been waiting, or had followed them and shot them down during or after the bust. But who? I didn't know. But I *did* know that if I looked in a mirror, I'd see the prize suspect. There was nobody left to tell the truth about my involvement. And that was very bad news for me.

Then I heard, far off in the distance, the sound of sirens. Someone had finally done their civic duty and called the authorities. I ran back towards the ramp, carrying the phone, slipped in a slick of blood, steadied myself and kept running, splashing through the puddles of water and crushing the little beasties that lived in them to paste under the soles of my DMs.

39

I tossed the phone into the back of the car, jumped into the driver's seat, and switched on the engine as the first blue light appeared at the corner a couple of hundred yards in front of me. I threw the car into reverse, revved up, dropped in the clutch, and the Cosworth shot backwards across the junction with the main drag. Luckily the street was empty, or else it would have been all over, there and then. I bumped the kerb on the far side, changed into first, and floored the accelerator. I powered round the Newington Butts roundabout, past the Tabernacle on my left, and into the second roundabout outside the College of Printing. All of a sudden there seemed to be police cars everywhere.

Right in front of me was a police Rover, stopped in the middle of the street. I swerved round it and saw another tearing along St George's Road in front of me. I bumped straight across the roundabout and turned into London Road, against the flow of one-way traffic. As I went, I heard the yelp of the siren on the Rover start up, and the car started in pursuit. Two more police cars were heading towards me down London Road, lights and sirens going. They both swerved to avoid the Cosworth. One scraped along a set of pedestrian railings in a shower of sparks like a Catherine-wheel flying off a nail.

Up ahead, St George's Circus was blocked with police vehicles, so I turned left into Garden Row, across St George's Road, sharp left into Geraldine Street, and round West Square, with the police Rover tight on my tail. I doglegged through to Brook Drive, turned right, and hit ninety up the narrow street between the lines of parked cars. Then left into Kennington Road, and right into Walnut Tree Walk, with the copper still keeping up. Right again into Lambeth Walk, shot the curve, accelerating all the time, then hard left by the pub into Lambeth Road and towards the river, foot hard down and the engine screaming in protest.

The car flew across Lambeth Bridge, and the Rover fell behind. There were more police cars east and west on Millbank, so I took the Horseferry Road turning, jumped the red lights by the hospital, and when I looked in the mirror it was to see a procession of headlights and flashing blue lights following me. I knew I had to lose them and find somewhere to lie low, or I was in serious trouble. I zig-zagged through Victoria and Pimlico, taking left and right turns randomly as they came, not worrying about traffic-lights or one-way systems, trying to lose the pursuing convoy. I knew that it was only a matter of time before I was going to be captured. Although nothing in the Met could keep up with the Ford I was driving, they had the numbers, and I could imagine that the radio waves were burning up as every copper in London was called into the hunt.

Eventually, more by luck than judgement, I managed to shake off my pursuers, and when I found myself on Chelsea Embankment, heading west, I tromped the accelerator down and the needle on the speedometer touched a hundred and forty as I sped along, with the river gleaming dully on my left. The road was clear ahead and I thought I'd got away clear, until another Rover, or maybe the same one, swerved out of a side road behind me and continued the chase. I shot across the hump at the junction by Battersea Bridge, and the car nearly took off. The Ford roared through the curves, still doing a hundred and twenty.

When I saw Lots Road coming up on my left, I took a desperate chance and hit the brakes and spun the car through the gap between the kerb and the bollards in the middle of the junction. The four-wheel drive and the ABS kept the car on the road, just. But, even so, I felt the nearside wheels lift off the tarmac and I thought for a second I'd lost it. But the wheels touched down again with a screech of rubber, and I was heading towards the gasworks at the top of the road.

The Rover's driver didn't do so well. I heard a scream of protest from *his* tyres as he tried to manoeuvre through the corner, but he didn't make it. The car's wing caught the bollard, and tossed it twenty feet into the air, turning it over with a crunch of tortured metal, then the police car rolled through the window of the shop on the corner in a shower of glass. I hoped the driver and his mate were OK. It wasn't their fault that the Met couldn't afford to come up with a car that could keep up with mine. Vorsprung Dork Technic. As they say.

I drove through to a council estate in Fulham, cut the lights, and eased the car into a space between two artics parked up for the night. I slid down lower in the driver's seat and waited. From time to time I could see the reflection of blue flashing lights in the windscreen of the truck in front of me, and I just sat and waited for them to find me. There was little point in doing anything else. If I kept moving, I knew I was done for. What I needed was some traffic to get lost in. I sat there for nearly an hour as the sky lightened and London came awake around me.

Eventually I plucked up the courage to move on. I drove sedately through Fulham to Kensington, and didn't see a single police car on the whole journey. I found an underground car-park that had just opened, and parked the Ford in a quiet corner on the lower ground floor.

I walked around until I found a seedy hotel with a 'Vacancy' sign lit in the front window. I booked in as Mr Smith, and paid cash in advance. A slovenly porter showed me to a single room furnished in regulation motel-issue cardboard furniture, with plastic shag-pile on the floor that smelled like cats had been fucking on it, and a battered colour TV with a dodgy horizontal hold, which was chained to the wall. But it was a sanctuary, if only a temporary one.

I made coffee from the complimentary makings laid out for me on the sideboard, and sat on the bed and got out my cigarettes. When I looked for my Zippo, I couldn't find it. It was the least of my worries right then, but somehow it seemed like a bad omen. I begged a book of matches from the woman behind the reception desk and went back to the room, where I stayed for most of the rest of the day.

The TV news was full of the story. Seven people shot to death in an underground loading bay. What did I expect? There was no mention of me or the chase. The police were obviously still looking. But, then, I knew I could count on that.

I stayed sitting on the bed as the day dragged on. It was grey outside, with a low cloud base stalled over the city. It fitted my mood perfectly. The weatherman on TV forecast heavy rain later, which suited me fine. I could use all the cover I could get. Twilight came early as the clouds persisted, and eventually about six I decided to fulfil my obligation to Brady and go and try and find out what had happened to Alfie.

40

I walked back to the car-park through the gloom, and
checked out the Cosworth. It hadn't been disturbed as far
as I could see. I got inside and found my lighter on the
rubber mat under the steering-wheel. Now, maybe that
was a *good* omen. I paid the fee and headed back to South
London. The sky was getting darker by the minute, and
the clouds seemed to loom even lower in the sky as I
went. One by one the street-lights clicked on, and I switched
on my headlights. But it hadn't started raining yet.

I parked the Cosworth in a side street off the Kennington
Road, one turning up from the cul-de-sac where Brady had
lived. On the corner, outside a pub, was a call-box. I
phoned Brady's number from there. I needed a quick shufti
round the drum, and more importantly I needed to know if
any coppers were hanging around. I knew that if they
were, they'd answer the phone. They always do. They
can't resist it. But no one picked up, even after I let it ring
twenty times.

I went back to the car and got the torch I always keep
in the glove compartment of any car I drive, for occasions
such as this, then sauntered down and turned into the cul-
de-sac and checked out the house. It was dark and deserted-
looking. I rang the front door bell, just in case, and was
ready to do a runner if anyone I didn't know answered.
But I came up with a nish again. Then I went down the
narrow alley at the side and through the picket gate and
into the tiny garden.

I tried the kitchen door and window, and the patio door. All three were locked. I looked up. The bathroom was directly above the kitchen. The soil pipe came out of the wall next to the window and descended through the paving stones to the sewers running below. The bathroom window had translucent glass at the bottom of the window, louvred glass at the top. So much for security, I thought. I put one foot on the kitchen window-sill and, using the frame and the pipe as a ladder, I started to climb.

The kitchen window was in shadow, but as I got higher, I was lit by a street-lamp opposite. It felt like a spotlight, and I felt like a bug on a snowball, but luckily no one was around to see. I kept hold of the pipe with one arm, and knelt on the narrow sill of the bathroom window and, using my free hand, pushed the panes of louvred glass out of their metal runners and into the room. There were three of them and to me the sound of them hitting the floor inside was as loud as an orchestra tuning up. But once again no one seemed to notice. I wondered if I was in a neighbourhood watch area. If I was, the neighbours were falling down on the job.

The gap I had opened was about eighteen inches deep, and I squirmed between, slipped, caught myself before I fell, and pulled myself through, hanging upside-down above God-knows-what before I could turn, arm muscles shaking, and dropped with a crash into a puddle of broken glass. I was breathless, and stayed where I'd dropped for a couple of minutes to get myself straight. As I crouched there, I listened for any sound outside or inside the house that said I had company, or was about to.

But there was none. Just a well of silence.

When I'd calmed down, I started through the house, leaving the lights off and using only the narrow beam of the torch, filtered through my fingers, for illumination. I was looking for something, anything. But if you'd asked me what, I wouldn't have been able to say.

I went through the two bedrooms upstairs. Nothing. Then I went down and started on the ground floor. I was standing in the living-room where Brady's party had been held, with the top drawer of the black wooden sideboard open in front of me, and the minutiae of home owner's insurance in my hand when the light in the room was switched on.

I froze, then turned slowly. Alfie was standing in the doorway, his hand still on the light switch. He was wearing a black Burberry over black sweat pants and black hi-top Reeboks. His face was drawn into lines that belonged to someone much older, and if ever a black man was pale, it was him.

'What are you doing here?' he said.

'Looking for you but I didn't think I'd find you,' I said, switching off the torch.

He didn't reply.

'You don't seem to find that strange.'

No reply again. And that was when I realised what the story was.

'Because a little bird told me you were in the hands of the bad guys,' I went on: 'kidnapped. Held to ransom. A hostage to fortune. But if you were – kidnapped, that is – it occurs to me that, under the circumstances, whoever kidnapped you wouldn't have let you go to wander hither, thither and yon to tell anyone who they were. So I really didn't expect you to walk in as if nothing had happened.'

'I live here,' he said.

'Not good enough,' I said. 'Not good enough by a mile.'

'I . . .' he said.

'So it further occurs to me,' I went on as if he hadn't spoken, 'that the only conclusion I can come to is that you were one of the bad guys yourself.'

He shook his head and looked down at the carpet.

'Don't try to kid a kidder, Alfie,' I said. 'You *were* there. Brady told me,'

He looked up at me. 'How . . .?'

'On the phone. He called me from his car. He was dying, but wouldn't call an ambulance or the police. He called me. Asked me to look out for you. What a fucking mug punter, eh, Alfie? Have a good laugh about that, did you?'

'No, it wasn't meant to happen that way.'

'So what way was it meant to happen?'

He said nothing, so I said it for him. 'You didn't think he was going to be there, did you? You thought he'd be safely out of the way somewhere, and I'd be doing the deal. So it was supposed to me that got gunned down.'

'No.'

'But it must have been a big surprise to one and all when Brady made an appearance.'

'They said no one would be hurt,' said Alfie. 'If Brady hadn't been there, nobody would have known about me.'

'I would,' I said. The words hung in front of us like a bad smell. 'And you must have known that Endesleigh and the rest were going to arrive.'

He just shook his head.

'Well, didn't you?' I insisted.

'I didn't know they were going to kill them.'

'I don't believe you.'

'I tried to stop them.'

'Bollocks. They'd have killed you too if you had. You just let it happen, didn't you?'

'Did he really ask you to help me?' All of a sudden he looked worse, if that were possible.

'Yes,' I said.

He started to cry. 'It should have been you,' he said.

I knew it. 'Why don't you sit down?' I said.

'I'll never sit down in here again,' he said. 'I'm finished here.'

'Please yourself,' I said. Funnily enough I didn't feel

anger or anything like that. More sorrow really. Whoever was behind this had used Alfie as much as he'd tried to use me. 'But why did you do it?' I asked.

'I needed money to get him away from all this.'

'All this what?'

'His job. The drugs and the drinking. It was driving him crazy.'

'Where were you going to go?'

He shrugged. 'Who knows? Anywhere. Anywhere warm and far away, where we could be together.'

Touching, I thought. 'So you knew that he was a policeman?'

'Sure.'

'He didn't know that.'

'He thought he was so clever. I've known for ages. You're not one, are you?'

'Not anymore.'

'But you used to be?'

I nodded.

'I thought so. You're like one.'

'I just got dragged into this mess. It wasn't my idea, believe me.'

He made no reply again.

'So he had no idea?'

'What?'

'What you were planning?'

'Of course not.'

'So what made you think he'd go with you? He was a policeman, and a straight one by all accounts, even if the job was driving him mad.'

'He loved me,' said Alfie.

'And love conquers all?' I said.

He didn't answer me again.

Then I asked the most important question of all. 'So who was there with you?'

'Lasky,' he said simply.

'Lasky?' I replied, and furrowed my brow. I knew the name – but from where?

'Gregor,' he said, and everything fell into place.

'The geezer at the party?'

He nodded.

'Runs restaurants.'

'Amongst other things.'

'Like protection?'

Again a nod.

'He's got a couple of geezers working for him drive a big red Yankee truck?'

'You know them?'

'Sure. We had a little run in last autumn. I remodelled the bodywork a trifle.'

'That was you?'

It was my turn to nod. 'So that's why he was visiting you the afternoon Brady and I fixed up the deal with Seeley and Hughes?' I asked.

One more nod.

'And I thought you two were carrying on.'

This time a shake of the head, but by then I didn't care.

'Brady didn't tell me he was there,' I said.

'He kept well out of sight. His men did the shooting.'

'How did he know where to go?'

He cocked his head in a puzzled way.

'Last night,' I said. 'When Brady was killed. How did you know where the deal was going down?'

'I don't know.'

'And how much was your cut going to be?'

'Around a hundred and fifty grand.'

'Not bad. And who has it now?'

'Gregor.'

'And the drugs?'

'Those too.'

'You're a very trusting soul.'

'I don't care about the money now. Not now that Brady is dead.'

'Do you know what he intends to do with the dope?'

'Sell it back.'

'But Seeley and Hughes are dead.'

'Not to them. To the people who employed them.'

Brady's big boys, I thought. Talk about honour amongst thieves. 'When?'

'Soon. Tonight maybe.'

'Where?'

'I don't know. I told you I'm not interested. But somebody is.'

'Who?'

'I don't know. I haven't been staying here. I couldn't bear it. I came round earlier and somebody was here. I saw them moving about?'

'Who?'

'Don't know. I didn't wait to find out.'

'Police?' I asked. I knew it hadn't been, because if it was they would have still been there. But I asked anyway.

He shook his head. 'The other police don't know about this place. Only the people on the squad knew, and they're . . .' He didn't finish the sentence. 'His official address is in Streatham, with his wife.'

'His wife?' I said. 'I didn't know he was married.'

'Surprised?' asked Alfie, a little fire returning to his demeanour.

It was my turn to shake my head. 'Not really. I just never thought about it.'

And that was about all the questions I had for him.

'So what happens now?' he asked after a minute.

'What happens now, is that you and I are going to Kennington nick, and you're going to tell them everything you know. Right?'

He hesitated, and I wondered if I'd have to apply some physical pressure. God knows, I didn't want to. He looked in a bad enough state as it was. 'All right,' he said. 'But can I just have a few minutes here. I won't be back, and I want to say goodbye.'

'Of course you can,' I said magnanimously. 'Take all the time you need.'

He walked out of the door and up the stairs.

41

I listened to Alfie walking about upstairs. His feet crunched on the broken glass on the bathroom floor, then moved across the hall to one of the bedrooms. Then there was silence, interrupted just once by a thump on the ceiling above me. I imagined him saying his last farewells to Brady's ghost. I lit a cigarette and went to the drinks cabinet and poured a large brandy. I thought I deserved it. I sat down and sipped the drink and finished the cigarette. After a few more minutes I went to the foot of the stairs. 'Alfie!' I shouted up. Nothing.

I walked up the first few steps and shouted again. Again there was no reply. I went up the rest of the way. The master bedroom door was closed. I tried the handle. It was locked. I knocked. 'Alfie!' I shouted through. Then I realised. 'Oh shit,' I said, and put my shoulder to the door. It was stronger than it looked. On the third try the lock splintered and the door burst open.

He'd rigged a rope from the light fitting in the centre of the room, climbed on to a chair, and kicked it away. That was the thump I'd heard. Where he'd got the rope from, Christ knows. Maybe he'd brought it with him, intending to kill himself all along, or maybe it was something that he and Brady used as a sex aid. Maybe the thought of going to the police with me had pushed him over the edge.

His face was suffused with blood and his tongue, which stuck out between swollen lips at an obscene angle, was the colour of liver that had gone off. I quickly felt for a pulse in his wrist. Nothing. I ran down to the kitchen, got a knife, went back up, put the chair back on its feet, climbed on it and cut him down. I loosened the rope from round his neck, and tried for vital signs again, but it was no use.

'You bastard,' I said. I could have kicked him, but he was past feeling any more pain.

So that was the only witness I could muster for my defence, gone down the fucking Swanee, and I was well and truly up it without a paddle. But at least I knew who was behind it all, and where he was based, so it looked like I'd have to sort it myself. And for that I needed a gun. And I knew exactly where one was. Or where one had been recently. One with my prints all over it that had tied me to the killing of a copper. At the least I could screw up that damaging piece of evidence, and at the most prove that I'd been working for Endesleigh.

Or die in the attempt.

42

I left Alfie on the floor, and went back to the car. I turned the house lights off as I went.

As I opened the door of the Ford and got in, a police Metro sped past me on the opposite side of the road, in the direction of the river. I saw the driver clocking me, so I belted up and switched on the engine and pulled away quickly. I looked over my shoulder and saw smoke coming from his tyres as he braked into a U-turn. Oh Jesus, I thought, not again.

As I put my foot down, the skies finally fulfilled their promise and opened. I put on the headlights and the wipers, and red-lined the rev-counter as I overtook a bus and headed in the direction of Kennington Park. In the mirror I saw the Metro's blue light come on, and I heard the whoop of the siren. That's all I need, I thought.

The lights were green by the park, and I turned left into Kennington Park Road and dodged through the thickening traffic heading for the Elephant. When I looked in the mirror, the Metro was gaining on me. I did a risky right by Kennington tube, and I was almost hit by a black cab as I did so. Then I started to cut through the back doubles, always trying to keep in the general direction of London Bridge. The rain was really hammering down by then, but the Ford stuck to the roads like a leech, and I blessed its permanent four-wheel drive again.

I crossed the Walworth Road and headed in the direction of the New Kent Road. The Metro was flagging, but still in sight. The problem with the streets I was using was that I had no chance to really build up any speed. As I turned into a street close to the Bricklayer's Arms, I saw that I was in a lot of trouble. There was some building work going on, and a cement lorry was manoeuvring to reverse into the site and drop its load, and was effectively blocking the street. I slowed down and the Metro turned into the street behind me. I let the car slow a little more, and banged on the steering-wheel in frustration.

Then I saw one way of escape. There was a skip opposite the entrance to the site. A workman in a bright yellow rain-slicker was pushing a wheelbarrow up the plank to dump some rubbish into it. There was another plank leaning against the skip, parallel with the first. As far as I could reckon, they were about as far apart as the wheelbase of the Cosworth. It was a chance in a million but I had to take it.

I slammed the Ford into second gear and literally stood on the accelerator. I hit the horn and the workman turned at the sound, and his mouth opened in a disbelieving O before he jumped off the plank and the wheelbarrow toppled to the pavement. I aimed the car at the planks, and whispered a prayer. The Ford was doing over a hundred MPH as it shot up the ramp the planks formed, and it took off over the skip. I ducked down low, as I knew that when the car hit terra-firma I could brain myself on the roof. The car seemed to hover in mid-air for a split second, and the engine screamed and the wheels spun as they lost contact with the planks. Then the back of the car dropped, and it hit the ground with a force that about broke my spine. There was a terrible grinding of metal and pieces of the car broke loose and clattered around it. It bounced once, then all four wheels smashed down, and I hit the brakes, and it skidded along the wet road surface. Even the ABS couldn't cope with that landing. As the car rocked to a halt, the Metro hit the planks, but having a narrower wheelbase, only the nearside set climbed the ramp, and it tipped over on its side and the front hit the skip hard. Pretty soon the Met would be sending me bills.

I put the Ford into first and pulled away. But the car was sick. Very sick. In fact it was about on its last legs. Or wheels. The steering was fucked, and the engine sounded like hell, and was throwing a ton of smoke out of what was left of the exhaust system. I needed a new car badly, and some way into the warehouse where the gun was.

And then, as the Ford limped into Great Dover Street, there, three cars in front of me, I saw exactly what I wanted. It was a dark-coloured Range Rover – I couldn't tell exactly what colour because of the torrential rain – this year's reg, sitting high above the other traffic. The rear-light clusters were caged in black metal crash bars, and I assumed the front was similarly protected. If I was going to need a battering ram, then this was it.

At the next junction the Range Rover went straight over into Marshalsea Road, while the cars between us turned right. Perfect.

I followed the Vogue. The rain was drumming down on the roof above me with a sound like a marching band, and I could see it turning to steam on the Cosworth's bonnet. The Range Rover slowed, and I suddenly pulled around and cut in front of it, and forced it to stop. I opened my door and got out into the driving rain.

Through the water-streaked windscreen of the Vogue, with the wipers beating out their cadence, I saw the pale faces of the occupants. A man was driving, a woman sitting next to him. He opened the driver's door. Bad mistake, I thought, in this town. *Never* open the door if some lunatic cuts you up. Just close all windows, lock all doors and hope for the best.

'What the . . .?' he said – and I grabbed the door handle and tugged the door open wide. Both the occupants were in evening dress. On their way to the opera, or dinner, or a party or something. I took hold of the silk lapels of his jacket and tried to pull him out into the rain, but his seat-belt held him in. I reached into the car and hit the release catch, then dragged him out. It was all done so quickly he had no time to resist, but the woman, a pretty brunette about thirty-five or so, let out a half scream and covered her mouth with her hand.

I stood him against the side of the car. The rain was coming down even harder then, and we were both soon drenched. 'I'm taking this,' I said.

'What . . .?' was all that he could say before I hit him in the stomach. Lowdown where it really hurts. He doubled up and slid down the slick side of the Vogue, and sat in a puddle of rainwater that had collected on the blacktop. By then the rain was so fierce that it was bouncing back off the road.

I left him there and went back to the vehicle. The woman was tapping in a number on the car-phone. Her fingers were trembling, and her face was the colour of newsprint. I put my hand over hers on the dial pad. Her skin was cold, and she jumped when I touched her.

'Don't,' I said as gently as possible. 'Get your coats and get out.' It wasn't the nicest thing I'd done lately. But then who was being nice to me?

The woman did as she was told, and reached into the back for a pair of stone-coloured mackintoshes that were resting on the back seat. Then she got out of the door on her side, put on her coat, and went round to the man. Behind us a couple of cars had drawn up, and I could see more pale faces peering out. Someone tooted his horn, but I ignored it. I pulled the driver out of the way of the back wheels and got into the Range Rover and shut the door. I put the stick into drive and pulled away. I was soaking wet and dripping all over the velour, so I put the heater on to full and switched on the blower. At the next corner I turned in the direction of London Bridge.

43

It took me less than fifteen minutes to get there, and I was still soaked to the skin as I turned into the service road. I drove up to the metal-roller door, got out and took a look around. The building was dark and deserted. The only sound was the rain, and the gush from a stream of water pouring down one of the walls from a blocked gutter beneath the eaves of the roof.

I knocked, but to no avail.

I went back to the Range Rover, securely belted myself in, and did a tight three-point turn so that the car was pointing away from the door. I switched to four-wheel drive, revved up hard until the whole car was shaking, and dropped the gear-stick into reverse. The rear of the Vogue hit the door with a shock that drove me back into the driver's seat and rattled it on its mountings. The back window imploded on impact and showered me with broken glass. I drove forward, then did the same again. I felt the door give on the second attempt, so got out to check it. The metal strips were bent and twisted, and one side of the door had sprung loose of its runners. The back of the Range Rover was a mess. The bars that protected it were bent all out of shape, and both sets of rear lights were gone. The drop down back door was a ruin, and the rear compartment was full of broken glass. They don't make them like they used to.

I got behind the wheel again, put the stick back into reverse, and let the Vogue creep up to the door. Once it was hard against it, I revved the engine. The car pushed against the door, and as I revved harder I heard the terrible squeal of metal on metal, and the door bent and finally gave. The body of the car pushed it out of the way, and finally I was inside the warehouse. I switched off the engine and sat still in the sudden silence. The bulb in one headlight had popped, and the beam from the other cut through the gloom like the eye of a Cyclops.

I put the car into forward gear and turned round and drove upwards to the fourth floor. I stopped it facing the Portakabin, headlight on the door. I left the engine running, got out, and tried the handle. It was locked. I went back to the Vogue, wrestled the damaged tailgate open, and lifted the carpet. Next to the spare wheel was a tool-box. Inside was a decent-sized screwdriver. I used it to jimmy open the door of the cabin. I leant in and switched on the light.

Inside it was much as I remembered. Table, chairs, filing cabinet, microwave, kettle, mugs, etc. Again I used the screwdriver to break into the filing cabinet. Inside the top drawer was the cardboard box. And inside the box, the special-edition Colt Commander Light Weight. I picked it out and weighed it in my hand.

I was about to pump a round into the breech, when a woman's voice from behind me said, 'Hold it right there, Nick.'

I nearly jumped out of my boots, and began to turn.

'Stand still. Now step backwards very slowly and place the gun on the table. No tricks. I'm armed.'

I thought I recognised the voice. 'Is this a joke?' I asked.

'Try something, and see how funny it is,' she said.

I took a chance and turned my head. I'd been right: it was Kylie. She was dressed in black boots, navy-blue trousers, and a short navy-blue reefer jacket buttoned up tight. On her head, pulled low over her blonde hair, was a black baseball cap, and over one shoulder was slung a black leather bag on a strap. The cap and the shoulders of her coat were spattered with drops of water. In her right hand was an ugly black revolver with a short barrel.

'Very fetching,' I said. 'Did you pick the gun to go with the outfit, or vice versa?'

She cocked the pistol. It made a nasty metallic sound in the silent interior of the cabin. I didn't know what the hell was going on.

'Hey,' I said. 'Remember me?'

'Shut up. Face the front and do as you're told,' she ordered.

I did as she said. I didn't want the gun going off. Could be nasty that. I walked slowly backwards until my thigh touched the edge of the table, reached behind me and placed my gun on top. Very slowly, very carefully, so that there could be no mistakes made.

'Now walk forward to the wall. Don't look round. Hands against it, feet apart. You know the drill.'

Once again I did as I was told. I assumed the position, as the Americans say. I stood off-balance, tilted forward, legs astride, with the weight of my body supported on my hands, against the wall in front of me.

Kylie came up behind me, kicked my legs further apart, and searched me. 'Turn around,' she said, when she was satisfied I was unarmed.

I pushed myself away from the wall and did as I was told. Kylie had stepped back, and she kept the gun on my mid-section. Cosy.

'So, what's the story?' I asked. 'I think I must have missed something.'

She changed the gun to her left hand and reached into her right-hand coat pocket and took out a leather folder and flipped it open. I'd seen one before. Loads of times. Had one myself once. 'Police,' she said, as if she needed to.

I couldn't believe it. 'Dear, dear, dear,' I said. 'They

get younger all the time.' Just to mask the surprise I felt.

She didn't reply.

'Kylie,' I said. 'What the hell is all this about?'

'My name's not Kylie. Detective Sergeant Patricia Shaw, drug squad.'

'And whoring's your Saturday job?'

'Undercover,' she said.

'Christ, you take your job seriously,' I said.

'I do.'

'I don't believe it.'

'What's not to believe?'

'You know what I'm talking about.'

'Do I?' she said in a scornful tone.

'Were you working for Endesleigh, too?'

She nodded.

'And he let you do that?'

'It was my decision.'

'Christ,' I said.

'Does it offend you? You certainly took advantage of the service. You're just a fucking hypocrite, like all men.'

'It doesn't offend me,' I said. 'But I thought it might offend you.'

'I've done worse.'

'Have you really?'

She nodded. 'So just shut up about it.'

'If you say so,' I said. 'You've got the gun.'

'Just remember that.'

'I will,' I said. 'But let the hammer down, will you. It's making me nervous.'

She didn't. 'You look like a drowned rat,' she said. 'Did you have trouble getting here?'

'Transport problems.'

'You certainly made a mess of someone's nice car,' she said conversationally. 'And the front door. If you'd let me know you were coming by, I'd've made sure it was on the latch.'

'I didn't know I'd be coming by at all,' I replied. 'How did *you* know?

'The lighter I gave you,' she said.

'What about it?'

'Take a look at it.'

I took it out of my jacket pocket. It looked like a lighter.

'Take it apart,' she said.

I separated the works from the case, as if I was going to fill it. When I looked closely, I saw that the case had a false bottom. It was good work. I would never have noticed unless I'd been told.

'Built-in transmitter,' said Kylie. I couldn't think of her as Patricia. 'You're on satellite.'

'Like Bart Simpson,' I said. 'And I thought you really cared.'

She didn't say anything at all to that.

'Why didn't you pick me up before?' I asked. It might have been better all round if she had.

'I lost the transmission. What did you do – spend all day underground?'

'The lighter did. In a car-park. I'm glad all this technology's not infallible.'

'Nothing is. I picked you up earlier, and I've been following you ever since.'

'And here we are.'

'That's right. So who were you going to shoot?' she asked, gesturing towards the Colt.

'What makes you think I was going to shoot anyone? It's evidence, isn't it? Makes me a murderer. You must know about that scam.'

'That's the least of your worries,' she said. 'You're also tied into another seven murders. Brady and the rest. There's a lot of people want to talk to you.'

'So I gathered, but I didn't kill them. Why should I? I had nothing to gain.'

'For the money and the drugs.'

'No,' I said. 'I agreed to help, but it got screwed up. I wasn't there last night. Not until later. Brady called me.'

'He called you?' she said incredulously. 'Why *you*?'

'Maybe he didn't think you could handle it, sergeant. And he wanted a favour.'

She ignored the snide comment. 'What sort of favour?'

I told her.

'Brady was a stupid bastard sometimes. I told him that queening around with some little rent-boy was dumb.'

'You were right,' I said.

'Well, if you know so much, who did kill them?' she asked.

So I told her that, too. Everything that Alfie had told me, and everything else I knew, right back to the pair who'd come to JJ's and mentioned Lasky's name.

When I'd finished, she looked at me. 'It was me at the house,' she said. 'I went in to see if I could find anything useful.'

'You scared him off.'

'So where is he now? I'd like to hear it from him personally.'

I told her what had happened at Brady's house.

'Didn't you call an ambulance or anything?' she asked.

'He was dead,' I said.

'So you just left him?'

'What was I supposed to do? Carry him round for good luck?'

'You're a cold-blooded bastard, Nick. So what were you going to do next?'

'Go and find Lasky. See if I couldn't put a spanner in the works.'

'So you *were* going to shoot someone?'

I shrugged. 'Depends,' I said. 'I just wanted to find

someone who could clear me.'

'And you were going on your own.'

I nodded. 'Who was I supposed to go with? I've been stitched up all along the line. Endesleigh, Brady, Alfie, Lasky. And even you. I was daft to get involved with this in the first place, and I'm getting well pissed off with it. It's about time I started stitching someone up myself. But I don't need to now, do I? Not now that you're here.'

'Is that right?'

'Course it is. All you have to do is get on your radio, put out a call for Lasky and his mob, call in some back-up, and Bob's your uncle.'

She shook her head. 'Not now you've told me what happened.'

'Meaning?'

'Meaning I'm going to find Lasky myself.'

'You're crazy.'

'Don't you think I can do it?'

'I don't know.'

'You don't think I'm a little too girly for the job?'

I didn't answer. Instead I said, 'Why?'

'Because the officers who were killed were my friends. My oppo's. I'm all that's left of this squad, and I intend to finish the job.'

'You could get killed.'

'That's a chance I'll have to take.'

'You're mad. There's a whole police force out there. Use them, for Christ's sake.'

She shook her head.

'But you're the only one who knows the truth about me.'

She smiled. 'I'm a valuable piece of merchandise, then. Maybe you'd better come too.'

I was speechless.

She smiled again. 'It makes sense, Nick.'

'And if I don't?'

'I'll cuff you up and leave you here, and come back for you later.'

'And what happens if you don't make it?'

'Someone will find you, eventually.'

I didn't like the way she'd said that last word. 'And if they don't?'

'You'll have to gnaw your hands off at the wrists,' she said, and smiled.

'Charming,' I said.

'So?' she asked. 'Are you coming or not?'

I thought about it. She was right. 'What the hell?' I said.

'I knew you would,' she said, and picked the Colt off the table and tossed it to me.

44

She had a car outside, blocking the service road. It was a little red Astra. We drove straight to Greenwich. What with the rain and the remains of the evening traffic, it took about an hour. With the help of her *A-Z* I found the address where Lasky had his office. It was in a mews off the main road, with garages on the ground levels, and flats or offices on the first floors. Mostly offices—so by that time of night, the mews was quiet. Kylie stopped the car and killed the engine and lights.

I peered through the water-streaked windscreen at Lasky's place. The building was in darkness. 'Want me to take a look?' I asked. I wasn't that keen, as I was just beginning to dry out properly.

'No, I'll go,' she said. 'Can I trust you?'

'To do what?'

'To do nothing.'

'Sure,' I said.

'You won't go?'

'I've nowhere *to* go.'

'You could go to the police.'

'Without you? No. They'll stick me in a cell. By the time I manage to convince them that something is up, it'll be over.'

'You don't have much faith.'

'Give me one good reason why I should.'

'So you'll stay here?'

'Like a faithful hound.'

'I won't be long.'

She took the keys out of the ignition – trusting soul – and opened the door. I grabbed her arm. 'Don't go getting killed,' I said. 'You're the only one who can get me out of all this.'

'I love you too,' she said, and went.

'I thought you just might, once,' I said to the empty interior of the car. I watched as her dark-clad figure merged with the rainy night and she vanished.

She was back in ten minutes. She climbed into the car and shivered, took out the keys, started the engine, and let the heater run. 'I've been round the back,' she said. 'There's nothing doing. The place is deserted.'

'Shit,' I said. 'What do we do now?'

'Wait.'

'But it might be happening right now.'

'If it is, tough shit. Just wait. Be patient. You've done it before. You must have.'

But not happily, I thought. Yet I had no choice. 'OK,' I said, and took out my cigarettes.

'No smoking in the car, please,' she said.

'Great,' I said, and rammed the packet back into my pocket, pulled up my collar, and sat and sulked. That'd teach her.

They arrived about an hour later. I recognised the motor. The same red truck I'd taken a baseball bat to. I was very lucky they'd never come back for revenge. They might get their chance for it sooner than they imagined.

'That's them,' I said, and looked over at Kylie.

She was busy clocking the truck as it moved slowly up the mews and parked. The lights went off and both front doors opened. I saw two figures walk across to the front door of the mews house, but I couldn't identify them. Lights came on behind the front door and then on the first floor.

'Let's go,' she said. 'You knock on the front door. I'll

go round the back. There's a staircase up to the first floor. I'll get in through there. With luck they'll separate.'

'And if they don't?'

'Busk it.'

I did as I was told. I gave her five minutes, then rang the doorbell. I heard footsteps on the stairs. One set. 'Who's there?' said a voice.

'Gregor?' I said, with a question-mark.

'Not here.'

'I've got to see him.'

'I told you he's not here. Who are you?'

'Sharman,' I said. 'Come on, open up. It's pissing down out here.'

'Never heard of you.'

'It's about last night,' I said.

'Do what?'

'You know.'

There was a moment's silence, then I heard the lock go and the door opened. It was the black geezer who'd come to JJ's that day. I saw recognition on his face, and I shoved my gun in it.

'Ssh,' I said.

'Who is it, Del?' said a voice from upstairs.

I touched the forefinger of my free hand to my lips.

'Del?' The voice had moved to the top of the stairs, then I heard the sound of breaking glass and a gabble of confused voices, followed by a moment's silence.

'Come on up, Nick,' said Kylie's voice. 'I've got him.'

I pushed Del towards the stairs. He snarled at me and I snarled back. 'Get the fuck up there,' I said. 'Or I'll break your arm.'

'You cunt,' he said.

I didn't say anything in reply, just pushed him again, and he went. We walked up a dozen or so steps and into the office. It was painted white, furnished with dark, expensive-looking furniture and thick maroon carpet. The door that opened on to the outside staircase was open, and a pane of glass was shattered. Kylie was holding her gun on the white guy – the same one who had come with Del to JJ's to demand protection. When he saw me, his eyes widened with surprise. I pushed Del over to join him, and shut the door to keep out the wet draught.

Kylie showed her ID. 'So, boys,' she said. 'You're the ones who killed my guv'nor last night.'

'Bollocks. Don't know what you're talking about,' said Del.

'Meet Del,' I said. 'Charmer.'

'Hello, Del,' said Kylie.

He spat on the carpet between her feet.

'Can't get the staff,' I said.

'So who are you?' said Kylie to the white guy.

'Terry,' I said.

Kylie looked suspicious for a second, then said, 'Are they the ones?'

'Correct,' I replied. 'We've danced before. Isn't that right, Terry?'

He sniffed.

'See,' I said. 'Articulate, isn't he? So where's Gregor tonight?'

'Who's he?' said Terry.

'Oh Jesus,' I said. 'He's one of those.' I walked over and stamped hard on the toes of his trainers.

He bent down and grabbed his foot with a cry of agony. 'Christ,' he said. 'You've broken my foot.'

I kicked him in the face hard. Blood and teeth flew and he crashed across the carpet, where he lay moaning. 'I'm not police,' I said. 'I don't have to play by their rules. And guess what? I don't give a fuck.' I looked at Del, and gave him my best Jack Nicholson look. 'I'm down for those murders,' I said. 'And more. But I didn't do them. I know that. You know that. She doesn't know that. But *you* are going to tell her. And if I have to rupture something,

something soft and important in your body, before you tell the truth, I'll do it. Get me?'

He got me. Thanks, Jack.

He looked at Kylie pleadingly. 'You going to let him threaten me?' he asked.

She didn't answer.

I chuckled – and I thought the chuckle owed more to Rutger Hauer than to Nicholson, but it worked.

'OK,' he said. 'But we never killed no one.'

'So presumably you killed someone,' I said.

He looked at me.

'Double negative,' I said, then shook my head. 'Never mind.'

By then he was *convinced* I was a nutter. 'I never,' he said. 'It was the others.'

'Who?' asked Kylie.

'Billy and Barry,' he said.

I shook my head again. 'Billy and Barry. Sounds like a comedy duo.'

'Don't laugh,' he said. 'They're fucking radio rental.'

'They must be,' said Kylie. 'Is Lasky selling the stuff tonight?'

'What stuff?'

'Don't fuck about, Del,' I said. 'We've been getting on so well up to now. You don't want to end up like your mate, do you?'

He looked over to where Terry was, still lying face-down on the carpet, leaking blood and spit on to the pile. Lucky the carpet was dark red and didn't show much.

'So is Lasky selling the stuff tonight?' asked Kylie again.

Del nodded.

'Good boy,' I said. 'Where and when?'

'Will you speak up for me?' Del said to Kylie.

She nodded.

Liar, I thought.

'At that poncey disco,' said Del.

'Where?' said Kylie.

'The Dealing Floor?' I said.

Del nodded.

Brady had been right.

'What time?' asked Kylie.

'Late. One, two in the morning.'

'Who's going to be there?' Kylie again.

'Gregor, Billy and Barry.'

'Not you?'

He shook his head. 'We're meeting tomorrow.'

'For your cut?' I asked.

He nodded.

'So what happened to the cash?' I asked.

'Gregor's got it.'

'Here?' I said.

He shook his head.

'You'd better not be lying.'

'Honest,' he said.

'You don't know the meaning of the word.' But it really didn't matter by then. I looked at Kylie. 'What now?'

'We go there.'

I looked at my watch. 'It's a while yet,' I said. 'What about these two?'

'What do you think?'

'Police?'

'No, not yet.'

'Kill 'em?'

She smiled a radiant smile. 'Good idea.'

Del looked like he was going to soil his underwear. I don't think Terry knew what was going on.

'Don't worry,' she said. 'Only joking.'

Del didn't look much happier.

'The garage,' I said to him. 'Is there a back entrance?'

He nodded.

226

'Got the keys?'

He nodded again.

'Gimme.'

'They're in my pocket.'

He was learning. 'Get them out slowly,' I said.

He reached into the pocket of his jeans, fetched out a set of keys, and tossed them to me. There were two Yale keys on the ring, and a big Chevrolet ignition key for the Blazer.

'Get up, you,' I said to Terry. 'And get down there.'

He lay where he lay and didn't move. I must have kicked him harder than I thought.

'Help him,' I said to Del. 'And no messing.' The look in Del's eyes said that messing was the furthest thing from his mind.

He did as I told him, and they went – Del supporting Terry. I led the way, backwards down the staircase, gun trained on them. Kylie followed. We opened up the small back entrance to the garage, and I found a light switch. It was empty of cars, cold and bleak, with a bench running the length of one wall. Water pipes ran up two of the other walls. I tried them. Solid. 'Find something to tie them with,' I said to Kylie.

'I've got my cuffs.'

'How many pairs?'

'Three.'

'You came prepared. Where are they?'

'In my bag in the car. I'll get them.' She was only gone a few minutes. I stayed with the boys.

We cuffed Del and Terry to the pipes. I found a roll of gaffer tape on the bench and tore off two strips. Del saw what I was doing. 'You can't gag him.' he said. 'He won't be able to breathe.'

'He'll have to breathe through his nose,' I said.

'He'll choke to death.'

'Tough,' I said. 'That's the breaks. It's more than the

227

break you gave those coppers last night.'

He was silent. 'What happens if you don't get back?' he asked.

That was just what I'd asked Kylie at the warehouse. I gave him the exact reply she'd given me. 'Gnaw off your hands at the wrists.' Before he could say anymore I slapped the gaffer tape over his mouth. I did the same to Terry. He groaned with pain as I did it. Like I said, that's the breaks.

I turned off the lights and locked the door behind me.

Before we left the mews, I unplugged the phones and crushed the plugs under the heel of my boot. I took the car and garage keys and dropped them down a drain in the street, and, just in case they did get away and had spares, I found a sharp, pointed letter-opener on the desk in the office, and punctured the tyres on the Blazer. It was hard going, as they were well oversized and felt to be about three inches thick, but eventually the truck settled on its rims with a satisfying hiss of air.

'You're thorough,' said Kylie as we got back into her car.

'I had thorough teachers,' I said. 'Let's go.'

45

'Are you sure you don't want to bring in a few colleagues on this one?' I said when we were in the car and moving.

'We've been through all that,' said Kylie.

'We could both end up very dead,' I remarked.

She shrugged.

'We don't know who's going to be there,' I said.

'Billy and Barry and Lasky,' she said.

'No, from the other side.'

'We'll worry about that when we get there.'

I was worried about it already.

'We sorted out those two easily enough, just now,' she said.

'I've got a feeling Billy and Barry might be made of sterner stuff. You didn't see what they did last night.'

'I saw,' she said, and her mouth set grimly.

'Yeah, course you did,' I said, and shut up.

We could see the Venice Tower from the south side of the river when we were still miles away from it. It shone like a rainbow beacon calling to us, as we made for Rotherhithe Tunnel. We got to the wharf about eleven o'clock, and parked where we could see the entrance to the club. It was still raining.

'I hope they're not already inside,' said Kylie.

There were only a few cars parked up around that side of the building. 'I know his motor,' I said. 'I'll check.'

I got out of the Astra and took a walk, trying to look inconspicuous. Lasky's XJS was nowhere to be seen. I went back to the car. 'I don't think so,' I said.

'So we wait,' said Kylie.

'Here we go again,' I said.

'Have patience.'

So I did – but twice I got out of the car to smoke a cigarette in the shelter of one of the old dock buildings. Finally, about half twelve, the Jaguar drove up, followed by a dark-coloured Mercedes 190.

'Here they are,' I said.

Lasky got out of the driver's side of the Jag, and a woman stepped from the passenger side. Two big men got out of the Merc. From a distance they looked twins. Tweedledee and Tweedledum. Billy and Barry without a doubt. I had to remind myself they weren't in the least bit funny. Lasky carried an oversized briefcase. We watched as they went into the entrance.

'Who's the woman?' asked Kylie.

'His girlfriend, I imagine. Fanny,' I said.

'I don't want to use that lift,' said Kylie. 'We might walk straight into them and, like you said, we don't know who's going to be there to meet them.'

'So?' I said.

'Let's try the front entrance.'

'You're the boss,' I said.

We went round to the main door, a forty-foot-high edifice of plate glass, engraved like the tomb of an ancient Egyptian. Inside was a sumptuous foyer paved with marble, complete with a uniformed security guard presiding over a desk full of telephones and a bank of TV security monitors.

Kylie banged on the door. The security man looked up, shook his head, and gestured that we were to go round the side to the club entrance. She banged again and he angrily repeated the gesture. She stuck her warrant card against the glass and pointed to it. He got up from the desk in an exaggerated way and came to the door and studied it. I swear his lips moved as he read it. He looked at her, then her ID again, and went back to the desk and touched a switch, and the door lock clicked. Kylie and I went inside. As the door closed, I heard the lock click behind us. The security guard got up and met us halfway across the foyer.

'Detective Sergeant Shaw,' said Kylie, showing her ID again. 'We need to get to the top floor.'

'That's what I was trying to tell you,' said the guard. 'You'll have to use the club lift. It's just round the corner.'

'No,' said Kylie. 'Can we get up there from here?'

He shook his head. 'It's against the rules,' he said. 'Employees only.'

'Bend the rules a little,' I said.

I knew what he was going to say. 'It's more than my job's worth,' he said.

'This is official police business,' said Kylie. 'It's not that we want to get in without paying.'

'Sorry, love,' he said.

'I'm not your love,' she said shortly. 'Is that the lift over there?'

'You can't . . .' he said – and I pulled the Colt out of my jacket pocket and stuck it in his face. I was doing a lot of that, that night, and enjoying it more every time.

'Just tell us,' I said.

He paled. 'All right, all right. You take the lift to the thirty-ninth, then walk up. You can get in through the emergency doors. There's a button on the outside opens them.'

'Great,' I said. 'See how gratifying it is to assist the forces of law and order. You'll be up for an OBE if you're not careful.'

He looked at the desk and the screens and the phones. I looked for a camera. There was one watching us from the corner of the foyer like a praying mantis. 'Any more security on?' I asked.

He didn't answer for a second and I saw the lie form in his eyes. 'No,' he said.

'Bollocks,' I replied. 'I think we're being watched,' I said to Kylie, and pointed at the lens.

'We'll have to risk it,' she said.

I could have made him turn the camera and screens off, but the chances were there a was a panic button he could operate without us knowing, so I wasn't going to let him get near the desk. 'Got that last pair of cuffs?' I asked her.

She took them from her bag. 'Where's the karsy?' I asked the guard.

'What?'

'Toilets.'

'Over there.' He gestured towards a plain door in one wall.

'Come on, then.' I pushed him across the expanse of marble and through the door. It was sumptuous inside, but even a sumptuous toilet has to have water pipes. I shackled him to a set, like I'd done with Del and Terry, first passing the chain connecting the cuffs behind the pipe. 'Somebody will be down to let you loose soon,' I said.

'You bastard.'

'It's been remarked upon,' I said, and went back to find Kylie. She was waiting by the lift, doors open.

'The phone rang,' she said.

'I hope it was just his mum wondering what he wants for his breakfast,' I said, but I doubted it.

We got into the lift and went up to the thirty-ninth floor. We came out on to a long, wide corridor carpeted in pale green. Halfway along was a fire door leading on to concrete stairs carpeted with nothing. We went up. At the top of the stairs was an unmarked door. Next to it was a red button. I pressed it and the door clicked softly. I pushed it open and we were in another wide corridor, carpeted in the same shade of green. I could hear music close by. Loud. Opposite was a door marked OFFICE. We went into the corridor and I listened at the office door. I couldn't hear a thing, but the music would have drowned out anything but the loudest voices. I tried the door handle. It was locked. I shook my head at her and we went down the corridor together towards the music.

We came out in the restaurant overlooking the disco room. It was pretty near empty, like the last time I'd been there, except for one table which was full. Sitting round it, clockwise, starting at six o'clock, were Fanny, one of the big geezers who'd got out of the Merc – Billy? Barry? – Gregor, the other big geezer – Barry? Billy? – next to him Derek, the manager of the club, beside two more strangers. One was a little fucker, with the expression of a dyspeptic stoat, and a suspicious bulge under the left armpit of his soft leather jacket, and the other a suave-looking face in a dark suit and a white shirt that shone brightly under the ultraviolet lights.

Kylie pulled me back out of sight, and put her mouth close to my ear so that I could hear her. 'Lovely,' she said. 'We've got them all together.'

'Gregor and Fanny I know,' I said. 'And Derek, the bloke who runs this place. And the two Gregor came in with must be Billy and Barry. But who's the fashion-plate and the little bastard next to him?'

'The fashion-plate, as you call him, is the biggest fish of all,' she replied with a look of satisfaction on her face. 'Kaplan, Anthony H. Owns a lot of real estate round here. Including most of this place. He was Brady's *numero uno* target. And now he's mine.'

'So how do you want to play this?' I asked.

'Quietly. With the minimum of fuss. They're not expecting us. We can take them down before they know what's happening.'

I admired her optimism, but I had severe doubts. 'If you say so,' I said. 'Quietly it is.'

'Let's do it then,' she said.

46

We walked together towards the table. It was covered with glasses and bottles. In front of Gregor was a briefcase. I assumed it was the one he'd brought with him, as they would hardly have had time yet to do the deal, what with getting the booze in and all. I had my hand on the Colt in my pocket. Kylie's right hand was inside her bag. In the other she carried her police ID. I put my arm around her. Although we weren't exactly dressed for a night of club culture, I wanted us to look as much like a carefree couple as possible. She looked up at me in surprise as I did it, and I winked. The music boomed, and the TV screens on the wall scrolled out currency values worldwide in ice-blue and yellow figures on a black background.

As we got close to the table, I let her go and stood behind Fanny. Kylie took centre stage. Where the table was situated was like the eye of the hurricane. The disco speakers had been cleverly placed so that it was possible to make yourself heard without screaming, yet no one closer than a couple of feet could hear a word. The most perfect place in the world to do a dirty deal in private. As we stopped at the table, everyone there looked up with varying expressions of recognition and surprise on their faces.

Kylie tossed her ID on to the table amidst the washing-up. 'Police,' she said. 'Everyone get your hands on the table. Now!'

Gregor started to stand up, and Kylie brought her hand

out of her bag with the revolver held in it. Gregor sat down again.

I pulled the Colt from my pocket. 'You heard her,' I said. 'Let's see them.'

One by one they obeyed. When I saw fourteen hands on the table, I relaxed slightly. It had been a lot easier than I thought. Mind you, our problems were just starting, but at least we'd won the first round on points.

'Then you're all going to stand up and go out through the restaurant to *your* office,' said Kylie, pointing her gun at Derek. Then, to Gregor, 'Is that the bag you brought in?'

He didn't answer right away. 'Well?' she demanded. He nodded. 'Where's the money?' Nobody said a word to that. 'Come on, where is it?'

'He's got it,' I said. Looking at Kaplan. 'Him or his minder.'

She moved the gun in Kaplan's direction. He stiffened.

'Here,' he said and pushed another bag out from under the table. It was about the same size as the one Gregor had brought.

'Good,' said Kylie. 'Nick, you bring that.'

I didn't like it. It was possible they were all armed. Even Fanny might have a little nickel-plated .22 keeping warm in her stocking top. There were too many of them, and too few of us. The fact that no one else in the room had clocked what was going on was the half-inch in which we were living. One nosy waiter or waitress raising a fuss could bring the roof down. I knew it, and I knew that Gregor, Derek, Billy, Barry, Kaplan *et al.* knew it too. I was beginning to wish more and more that Kylie had called for back-up.

'Right,' said Kylie. 'When I tell you, stand up slowly, keeping your hands where we can see them, and move through the restaurant to the office. Don't bunch up. Don't speak. And look happy. It's party time, and we're all friends here.'

I moved so that I had an unrestricted view of Kaplan's minder, but I also kept throwing glances at Billy and Barry, whichever one was which. The sooner we had them confined and unarmed the better.

I was so busy trying to do three things at once that I didn't notice a woman come through the main door of the club, down into the disco, and head in our direction. I didn't notice her until she was almost at the table. As she passed into my peripheral vision I looked at her sharply, looked away, then did a classic double-take. It was Jools.

She was dressed up to the nines in something short and sexy in white. But she looked like hell. Like someone who'd seen their worst dream come true whilst they were awake, and didn't like it one little bit. She was carrying a leather tote-bag over her shoulder and her right hand was inside it, like Kylie's had been in hers earlier, and it took me a fraction of a second to realise why. A fraction of a second too long. By then it was too late. Out of it she produced a Colt automatic. The twin of the one I was carrying.

'You bastards!' she screamed, loudly enough to drown out the music. She aimed the gun at Gregor, and fired. The bullet hit him in the middle of the chest. Jools turned the gun on Fanny, who was starting to rise to her feet, a scream already growing in her throat. A .45 slug chopped the scream off and she crashed across the heavy sitting next to her, in a tangle of arms and legs and long blonde hair.

Kaplan's minder came to his feet, too. With practised ease he drew a heavy revolver from under his jacket and shot Jools just above the right breast. Then I saw the gun begin to move in Kylie's direction.

He'd done it wrong. He wasn't to know. No one was. He was protecting his boss. That was his job. He should have shot me or Kylie first, and left Jools for later. It was the most expensive mistake he'd ever made. I shot him twice. Once in the throat, once lower in the chest, as quickly as I could pull the trigger. He tumbled backwards over his chair, his legs came up, and the table went flying in a shower of booze and glass and three hundred thousand quid's worth of top-quality cocaine in a briefcase.

Then it was chaos. There were screams as the few punters in the place hit the floor, or decided that Stringfellow's probably had a better ambience and made for the exit. The gaff was blown. Well and truly. And I knew that Kylie and I could die in the confusion. I fired a couple of shots in the direction of the table, and grabbed Kylie and threw her bodily behind a settee facing a low table nearby. She was my insurance. I badly needed her alive, not in a refrigerated drawer in the mortuary, where she couldn't talk. As we hit the deck, the door that led from the restaurant to the emergency exit we'd used burst open, and two security guards came charging in, both holding what looked suspiciously like UZI carbines.

The Billy/Barry who hadn't collected Fanny's body in his lap came up armed and fired in their direction. A hole blossomed in the leading security man's uniform shirt, and he did a perfect forward somersault to land in a heap on the carpet of the restaurant. His UZI spun through the air, slid across the glass dance-floor, bounced off the front of the DJ's booth and back down the wide steps, to land about twenty feet from the sofa behind which Kylie and I were crouching.

Meanwhile, the other guard triggered a spray of heavy-calibre bullets that zipped up the shooter's body horizontally, like a row of buttonholes, and danced him backwards in our direction, until his legs collapsed and he fell and lay still. The guard who had fired dropped behind a restaurant table for cover.

Apart from the sound of Eric B and Rakim coming

through the speakers at mega Dbs, all was quiet for a moment.

So there we were. Split into four factions. Kylie and me behind the sofa, between the disco and the main exit via the lift. Kaplan and Derek hiding somewhere in the debris of the table. Armed? Who knew. But I had to assume so. Then there was the surviving Billy/Barry. Armed definitely. Pissed off, too, I bet. And, finally, between the disco and the other exit, a security guard with an automatic weapon. There were also two cases. One containing a fortune in cocaine. The other filled to the brim with the equivalent in cash. To the victors go the spoils.

I sat for a second and tried to work out how many bullets were left in the Colt. Not many. I needed another gun. There were plenty lying about. It was like the bargain basement at Woolwich Arsenal. Blue spot day.

My ears were still ringing from the music and the gunfire. I leant close to Kylie. 'You OK?' I asked.

She made an 'O' with thumb and forefinger. She looked pleased. Maybe what had just gone on top was her idea of quiet. Maybe she was just relieved to be alive. I know I was. But for how much longer?

I peered round one side of the sofa. Kylie did the same on the other. From behind the overturned table Derek appeared, pushing a case in front of him. It was the money. He didn't have a gun. Kylie fired twice and hit the case, and he ducked back, leaving it on the carpet. Billy/Barry popped his head up and fired at us, but missed. The bullet ripped through the sofa. Kylie took a pot-shot at him, but with no apparent effect.

At that point the second security guard decided to get back into the game. He'd been lucky so far. He stood up and sprayed the place with the remains of the UZI's clip. Glasses flew, the sofa absorbed a couple more bullets, half a dozen or so TV screens imploded into oblivion, taking the exchange rates of the mark and yen with them, the DJ booth suffered a mortal wound, and the music stopped dead – but no one was hit.

I looked over at Kylie. She was using a speed-loader to fill the cylinder of her gun. 'Give me more fire,' I yelled. 'That fucker's going to get lucky and kill one of us if we're not careful.'

She leaned round the far end of the sofa and fired two shots into the restaurant. The guard dropped, then popped up again, UZI blazing and I emptied the Colt at him. Got him, too. He tumbled backwards, and the last of his bullets hit the ceiling, blowing bulbs in the fancy light displays.

I was out of ammunition, and had no spares, I needed another gun desperately. I dropped the Colt and went for the first guard's UZI. The twenty feet between the sofa and the gun seemed like twenty miles. I heard gunfire behind, but couldn't tell if it was aimed at me or if it was Kylie giving me cover.

I scooped up the machine-pistol and rolled behind the DJ's booth. The DJ had scarpered. Who could blame him?

I stuck my head round and took a squint at what was going on. The place looked like a battlefield. A battlefield illuminated with twinkling lights and a big multi-faceted glass ball spinning slowly in the middle, splashing everywhere the reflection of hundreds of spotlights aimed at it through the smoke from the firearms. Somewhere, someone was screaming. A highpitched wail that wouldn't stop. I stood up and crouched behind the booth. I fired a single shot in the direction of the table. Kylie looked around and waved. I didn't wave back. Billy/Barry came up and fired at me. I switched to full automatic and fired half a clip. It only took a second, and the gun was hard to control. Billy/Barry came up to return fire and Kylie gut-shot him. He stood for a moment with a look of amazement on his face, then dropped his gun and slowly crumpled to the floor.

Silence reigned.

Kylie looked over in my direction, and I left my cover and ran to her. When I slid down beside her she looked round the sofa and shouted, 'Kaplan! Derek! It's all over. Throw out any weapons you have, and stand up slowly. We won't shoot.'

There was a cry from behind the sofa and Derek came slowly to his feet, hands aloft.

'Where's Kaplan?' said Kylie.

'Here my dear,' said a voice from our left. 'Now drop your weapons both of you. I *will* shoot.'

Kylie and I looked round as one. Somehow Kaplan had managed to weasel himself from behind the table in all the excitement, and was now standing on the glass dance-floor, still immaculate, but holding a small revolver as a fashion accessory.

'I mean it,' he said. 'Drop the guns.'

I looked at Kylie. She looked at me. We both shrugged and obeyed.

'You,' he said to me. 'Fetch me the cases. No tricks, or the young lady dies.'

I went over to where Derek was still standing amongst the carnage, and found both cases.

'Bring them to me,' ordered Kaplan. I did. 'Now slide them across the floor. Gently.'

I slid the first one over to him. I knew he was going to kill us. Behind him the huge plate-glass window, riddled with bullets, creaked in the wind that rushed round the top of the tower. I looked down through the floor. The streets were black with firefly lights. It might be grim living down there, but it was better than dying up here.

'Come along,' said Kaplan. 'Don't keep me waiting.'

The bag was heavy, but I was facing a loaded gun, and was desperate. I swung it up and at him. He moved to one side to avoid it, and laughed. The bag hit the window with a crash and burst open. It was the money bag. Cash fell everywhere.

'You bloody fool,' he screamed, and I thought he was going to fire. I tensed myself for the impact but it didn't come. He was too worried about the money. He backed away, still brandishing the gun. 'I'm going to enjoy killing you and your slut. But first re-pack the case.'

'Slut,' I retorted. 'It was young lady a moment ago.'

'Just do it,' he said more calmly, but I could see a vein popping under the skin of his forehead.

I moved to do as he told me, but before I could take a step, the window began to vibrate violently, and with a screech like a million banshees it began to crumble down on itself. He looked up at it in disbelief and tried to run, but it was too late. With a sound like the roar of a waterfall, it broke. Huge shards, fifteen, twenty feet long, as heavy as pianos and as sharp as knives, fell down on him, slicing his body into strips as if he'd stepped into a giant food-processor. The wind and the rain tore through the gap and picked up the money and swirled it round the interior of the huge room, and sucked it out to scatter it across the city.

I went back to Kylie. 'Jesus,' she said, 'Did you ever see anything like that?'

'Not until now,' I said over the keening of the wind. 'Don't you think you'd better get that back-up now? I'm sure Derek will let you use his phone.'

Derek was still where we'd left him, hands in the air, looking in horror at the remains of his ex-boss. Kylie grabbed him, and together they went through the restaurant in the direction of his office.

I retrieved the empty Colt Commander I'd dropped, then sifted through the debris around the table and found the gun that Jools had used to kill Gregor and Fanny. I'd been right. They were identical. I checked the serial numbers: they were consecutive. The one Jools had brought was the higher number. Just like Chiltern had said. I went to look at the rest of the damage that had been done. The two security men were alive, but barely. Billy and Barry were both deceased. I wondered if I'd ever find out which one was which. Likewise dead were Fanny, Gregor and Kaplan's minder.

Jools was sitting in a corner. She'd pulled herself up into a sitting position with her back against a wall. Amazingly she was still alive, but I could tell she too was dying. Her skin was almost transparent, the colour of fresh milk, and clammy-looking. She was holding on to the wound above her breast with both hands, as if to keep her life inside intact. But they were scarlet with blood and it was still seeping through her fingers, and had soaked the bodice of her white dress.

'Cold,' she said. 'It's so cold in here.'

It was true that the temperature had dropped like a stone when the window went, but I didn't think that was the kind of cold she was feeling. I took off my jacket and draped it round her shoulders.

'Are they dead?' she asked in a small voice.

'Which ones in particular?'

'That bastard Gregor and his tart.'

'Yeah. You did for them. Why, Jools? Why did you do it?'

'Remember that party?' she asked. 'At Brady's house.'

I nodded.

'After Roy hit me, I went upstairs. She was there. Fanny. Wanted to be my friend. Telling me what bastards men are, as if I didn't know. She told me that if I wanted to get back at him I was to get in touch.'

'And you did.'

'Yes – after you dropped me off that day. Gregor knew there was a deal going down, I only had to find out where the meet was going to be and let him know.'

'Christ, Jools. You shouldn't have done that,' I said.

'I know. I know she was just using me. I didn't know anyone was going to get killed. I just wanted them to steal

243

the stuff. Hit Roy where it hurt.'

'And you did.'

'She told me to go back to Roy. Tell him I was sorry. Beg his forgiveness. You know the sort of thing. It worked, too. He was a sucker for all that.' She coughed and I saw blood in her mouth. 'He slapped me around a bit, then forgot all about it. He didn't care really. As long as I was there, like a piece of property. Then I spied on him. I was quite good at it. I found out where the meet was going to be, and told Gregor.' She started to cry. 'I loved him really,' she said.

'I know,' I said. 'I know you did.' I showed her the gun she'd used. 'Where did you get this?' I asked.

It took a moment to register, then she remembered. 'Pat Hughes got it. He bought two of them off a mate. A pair. They'd been nicked from somewhere.' Her voice was getting smaller, and I could hardly hear for the roar of the wind entering the broken window. 'He gave one to Roy. It was like a joke. No, not a joke. You know what I mean. Partners with matching guns. Like twins.'

'I know what you mean,' I said.

'It was in his drawer. I never fired a gun before today.'

'You did all right,' I said.

'Why do you want to know?' she asked.

'I got hold of the other one. The one Hughes kept.'

'How? Where?'

'Someone used it to shoot a copper a while back.'

'That sounds like Patsy Hughes. He always was a mad bastard.'

'How did you know Gregor would be here tonight?' I asked.

'That bitch told me. She thought I wanted some money. I couldn't take money, Nick, you know that. It was the last straw really. Her offering me money.'

'I know,' I said.

'But what about you?' she asked. 'What were you doing

here? And who were you with?'

'Long story,' I said.

'Aren't they all,' she replied, and her face twisted in pain. She was going fast. She opened her mouth and a great bubble of blood and saliva formed between her lips. She was dying, and taking it hard, and there was nothing I could do. She let go of her chest and grabbed my arm to pull me close. I went. The bubble in her mouth kept bursting and reforming, only to burst again as she tried to speak, and tiny drops of blood spattered on to her face and mine.

'Nick,' she said with great effort. 'We could . . .' And that was the last thing she ever said. She slumped back against the wall and lay still.

I wondered what she'd wanted to say, but I'd never know.

I took her hand off my arm, laid it back across the wound and tucked my jacket more securely round her.

A moment later Kylie came back through the restaurant and said, 'There'll be ambulances here in a minute.'

'Too late for her,' I said, and went looking for a packet of cigarettes.

More Compelling Fiction from Headline

Written in Blood

Caroline Graham

'Graham has the gift of delivering well-rounded eccentrics, together with plenty of horror spiked by humour, all twirling into a staggering *danse macabre*' *The Sunday Times*

It is clear to some of the more realistic members of Midsomer Worthy's Writers' Circle that asking bestselling author Max Jennings to talk to them is outrageously ambitious. Which is why Gerald Hadleigh, who knew Jennings many years before and for whom the prospect of seeing him again is the most appalling he can imagine, does not challenge the proposal. But, astonishingly, Jennings accepts the invitation and before the night is out Gerald is dead.

Summoned to the well-heeled village, Chief Inspector Barnaby finds that, despite the fact Hadleigh lived within a stone's throw of most of them, the polite widower was something of a mystery to his fellow group-members: as witnesses to his final hours they are little help. But the one thing they all agree on is that on the night of his murder Gerald was a deeply troubled man. The obvious cause of his distress was their guest speaker. So why did the wealthy and successful Max Jennings travel to Midsomer Worthy to talk to a small group of amateur writers? And, more to the point, where is he now?

'A wonderfully rich collection of characters . . . altogether a most impressive performance' *Birmingham Post*

FICTION / CRIME 0 7472 4664 5

Also available from Headline

WHEN DEATH COMES STEALING

A Tamara Hayle Mystery
'A riveting, emotional page-turner of an ending. An excellent debut novel' *Booklist*

Valerie Wilson Wesley

'Wesley is one of very few black women writers writing in this genre . . . a welcome new voice and a fresh point of view'
USA Today

Tamara Hayle fell in love with DeWayne Curtis when she was too young to know any better. The result was a disastrous marriage and Jamal, now fourteen. A private investigator, the last thing single mother Tamara wants back in her life is her shady ex-husband, but when he begs her to help him through some serious trouble she can barely refuse. For his eldest son has died a violent death and DeWayne's sons are the only humans he seems genuinely to care about, apart from himself. Then five days later there's another killing. And Tamara realises that unless she does something, and quick, her own son is next on a killer's list . . .

'Quick and often funny . . . reads like a successful collaboration between Terry McMillan and Sue Grafton' *Kirkus Reviews*

'Grips you by the throat and never lets go until the last spine-tingling word . . . a well-created novel with a poignant message that resonates long after the mystery is solved'
Bebe Moore Campbell

FICTION / CRIME 0 7472 4759 5

A selection of bestsellers from Headline

OXFORD EXIT	Veronica Stallwood	£4.99	☐
BOOTLEGGER'S DAUGHTER	Margaret Maron	£4.99	☐
DEATH AT THE TABLE	Janet Laurence	£4.99	☐
KINDRED GAMES	Janet Dawson	£4.99	☐
MURDER OF A DEAD MAN	Katherine John	£4.99	☐
A SUPERIOR DEATH	Nevada Barr	£4.99	☐
A TAPESTRY OF MURDERS	P C Doherty	£4.99	☐
BRAVO FOR THE BRIDE	Elizabeth Eyre	£4.99	☐
NO FIXED ABODE	Frances Ferguson	£4.99	☐
MURDER IN THE SMOKEHOUSE	Amy Myers	£4.99	☐
THE HOLY INNOCENTS	Kate Sedley	£4.99	☐
GOODBYE, NANNY GRAY	Staynes & Storey	£4.99	☐
SINS OF THE WOLF	Anne Perry	£5.99	☐
WRITTEN IN BLOOD	Caroline Graham	£5.99	☐

All Headline books are available at your local bookshop or newsagent, or can be ordered direct from the publisher. Just tick the titles you want and fill in the form below. Prices and availability subject to change without notice.

Headline Book Publishing, Cash Sales Department, Bookpoint, 39 Milton Park, Abingdon, OXON, OX14 4TD, UK. If you have a credit card you may order by telephone – 01235 400400.

Please enclose a cheque or postal order made payable to Bookpoint Ltd to the value of the cover price and allow the following for postage and packing:

UK & BFPO: £1.00 for the first book, 50p for the second book and 30p for each additional book ordered up to a maximum charge of £3.00.

OVERSEAS & EIRE: £2.00 for the first book, £1.00 for the second book and 50p for each additional book.

Name ....

Address ....

....

....

If you would prefer to pay by credit card, please complete:
Please debit my Visa/Access/Diner's Card/American Express (delete as applicable) card no:

Signature .... Expiry Date ....